A SWEET

PARIS, PUMPKINS, & PUNS

MARION DE RÉ

Copyright © 2024 Marion Thomas

Cover design by House of Orian

All rights reserved.

No part of this book may be reproduced or used in any manner without the prior written permission of the copyright owner, except for the use of brief quotations in a book review. Any use of this publication to "train" generative artificial intelligence (AI) technologies to generate text is expressly prohibited. Any unauthorized distribution or use maybe be a direct infringement of the author's rights and those responsible may be liable in law accordingly. For permission contact: marion@marionderewrites.fr

This is a work of fiction. Names, characters, businesses, places, events and incidents are either the products of the author's imagination or used in a fictitious manner. Any resemblance to actual persons, living or dead, or actual events is purely coincidental.

Paperback ISBN: 9798327931152

Ebook ASIN: B0DBJ82LVF

How About A Free Story?

Join my newsletter and receive a free story about two work enemies who get stuck together in the archive room of the museum they work at!

What to expect:

New Orleans setting and French references
Enemies to lovers
Workplace Romance
Cinnamon roll hero
Stuck together
Century-old love letters

Start Reading Now!

Heat level: Closed door, kissing only

Cursing: Mild (bible swears)

Notable tropes: Fake Dating, Cinnamon roll hero, French hero

Triggers: Loss of a parent in the past

Style: First person present, dual POV

Stress level: Low

Ending: HEA

To my own French Cinnamon Roll hero

Chapter 1

Hazel

"Great news! You're going to Paris," Jeff announces while flashing his million-dollar smile.

Okay. I might be exaggerating. As the editor-in-chief of an online food magazine, Jeff hardly makes millions. Though I know for a fact that he spent a small fortune on that new smile of his.

Wait, did he just say Paris?

He stares at me expectantly.

"Paris? Me? I thought Janet was going." She's the more senior writer between the two of us.

"Yeah," he says, scratching his forehead. "Well, Janet got engaged last night, so that kind of threw a wrench in our plans."

I frown. "I didn't even know she was dating."

"The whole thing happened pretty fast, apparently."

"Why can't she still go? Isn't it just a week-long trip?" I haven't paid much attention to the discussions around the Paris excursion since I knew I wasn't being considered, but I've heard Janet brag about spending a week in Paris with a list of ten restaurants to sample and critique.

"Well, yes and no. It's one week for starters, but more than that, I'm looking to deploy someone there permanently. Our French section garners half of the website's traffic, and I'm looking to develop it. Since you're the only team member without, um, *roots* here, I figured you'd be the perfect candidate."

Translation: the only one without a boyfriend or husband. Thanks for the reminder, Jeff.

He raises his eyebrows. "So, what do you think?"

"Wait. Do I have to give you an answer now?" How could I make such a big decision when I haven't even processed his offer yet? Moving to Paris, *permanently*? I need more time. He can't ambush me like this.

"The restaurant reservations are all for next week. Of course, I can always send someone else—even Janet—but I'd rather it be someone who might be interested in relocating to Paris after the New Year. Someone in need of a fresh start. This first week would be a chance to dip your toes into the Seine, so to speak. See if you could envision yourself working there. Naturally, the transfer would come with a great relocation package and a promotion."

I nod. Okay, that I can do. I never make good decisions on the spot. I need time to digest the idea before committing. "I'll think about it."

"Take the rest of the day off," Jeff says, clasping his hands together. "And call me if you have any questions."

Someone in need of a fresh start. The only team member without roots. His words echo in my brain as I pick up my stuff and stride out of the building. He's not entirely wrong. My breakup with Neal hit me hard. Coming back from that dark place wasn't easy, but I did it.

I think.

The truth is, I've learned to appreciate being single. Maybe it's just not my time. I admit, I did try to force it at first. I've been on blind dates, suffered through double dates, set up an account on dating apps—the works. And I'm telling you, being stood up after squeezing into an uncomfortable shapewear and shaving your legs is *not* fun. Now that I've chosen to let it go, I'm much happier. This is the time to focus on myself and my career. My season of love will come . . . Probably.

I step outside, stifled by the warm Floridian air as I hop in my car to drive home. Soon, I pull in front of the apartment I share with my sister. Hey, that's a root!

Ivy is a nurse at a nearby hospital, and this week, she's working the night shift. When I push the front door open, she's eating breakfast at the kitchen table.

"Watchadoinhere?" she asks through a mouthful of food.

Dropping my keys in the entry bowl, I kick my shoes off and amble up to her.

"Jeff wants me to go to Paris."

Swallowing her oatmeal, she plasters a big smile on her face, which reminds me just how beautiful she is. She tucks a lock of hair behind her ear as she gapes at me.

I've always been jealous of her hair. Hers is dark brown and wavy with copper highlights when mine is just a single shade of dull brown. You know those pictures on Pinterest that pop up when you search for hairstyles? Well, my sister could be one of those models. Her waves are sleek and shiny, and the rest of her is just as gorgeous. Of course her boyfriend doesn't feel the need to move to the other side of the world. Plus, she's a true Floridian who sports a bikini body all year long.

"Really?" she squeals.

I sigh, sitting down across from her. "Yeah. To try out restaurants for a week and write reviews, but also in the hopes I might move there."

"What?" she exclaims. Her face and tone don't carry the shock I expected. They're more excited. "That's amazing."

"Ready to ship me off, are you?" I sneer with a sarcastic edge.

She cocks her head to the side. "This is Paris we're talking about! Who wouldn't want to live there? I mean, sure, I'll miss you like crazy, blah blah blah. But *Paris*! The City of Lights, the romance capital of the world. And the Frenchmen." She licks her lips. "Haze, you deserve a good, hot Frenchman after what happened with Neal."

"You mean, after my boyfriend of two years dumped me to open a surf shop in Australia?"

She winces.

Yeah, 'cause that happened. As if he couldn't have opened one right here in the Sunshine State. But that's not even the worst part. When he told me about his plan, I naively thought he was asking me to move to Sydney with him. While it wasn't ideal, we'd been dating for a while and were pretty serious. But when I asked about it, he said, "Hazel, you hate everything about sports. What would you do in a surf shop? Eat the boards?" Then, he patted me on the back and laughed. *Laughed.*

He's not wrong about the sport thing, and I admit, I am a curvy girl. But what can I say? My job requires me to eat.

"I don't know, Ivy," I mutter as I examine my nails, which are clearly in need of a manicure. "It's just so sudden."

She puts her spoon down and fixes her dark-green eyes on me. "You know the saying. When life gives you lemons, make lemonade. Well, when your job gives you the chance to go to Paris, score yourself a French guy with a beret and say *merci*."

I burst into laughter. "As if that would ever happen. Are you crazy? Everyone is so skinny over there. If I can't get a man here, how on earth am I going to compete in Paris?"

"Exactly," she says, scooping up the last of her oatmeal. "You'll be exotic. French people love food. No, they *worship* it. I'm sure they don't mind a few curves."

I force a smile, but it falters. "Yeah . . . I guess."

Her shoulders drop. "Oh, come on. Think about all the fun you'd have there. Not only for a week, but imagine living there. All the amazing food, real bread that's crunchy on the outside but fluffy and warm on the inside, crêpes—you love crêpes—strolling on the Champs-Elysées, watching the Eiffel Tower sparkle at night, the incredible shopping you'd do there, the architecture. And did I mention the hot Frenchmen?"

She's got a point. I can almost picture myself wearing a striped sweater and a beret as I window-shop at the Galeries Lafayette, an accordion playing in the background. Quite a step up from Sawgrass Mills. It would be a fresh start, and except for Ivy, I really don't have anyone here. My only friends are Ivy's. Or Neal's. And guess who they sided with during the breakup? I don't care about finding a French beau, but I'll give Paris a try. For the food, the shopping, and the centuries-old architecture. *And* to see the Eiffel Tower sparkle at night. And anyway, I don't have to agree to the permanent job posting afterwards if I don't like it. I have nothing to lose.

"But what about you?" I ask, my eyebrows furrowed. "There's the apartment. You can't pay the rent by yourself."

She grimaces. "Well, Dan already lives here half the time, and he's been talking about us moving in together, so . . ."

I smirk. "So, it's the perfect opportunity to get rid of me?"

Her emerald eyes widen. "No! Of course not. I was just—"

I breathe a chuckle. "Relax, Ivy. I know what you mean. These past months haven't exactly been great for me. You're right. Maybe a change of scenery would do me some good."

She flashes me a bright smile. "You know what Audrey Hepburn says in *Sabrina*. Paris is always a good idea."

Chapter 2

Hazel

Paris is nothing like I expected. My sister, along with every American tourist guide ever, are all big fat *liars*. The city is dirty, the whole place smells like tobacco smoke, and I have yet to see a single man wearing a beret! Yes, I know I said I didn't care about French guys, but I figured it wouldn't hurt to look. Turns out, I was right, because there is nothing to see.

Instead of food critiques, I should be writing an article entitled *Paris: Reality vs Expectations*. Because, people, Hollywood got it wrong. Dead wrong.

To top it all off, there's a national strike going on—that cliché was spot on—which means demonstrations are taking place in the streets. They even vandalized the shop windows on the Champs-Elysées. Thankfully, I was able to take a stroll there earlier this week before the vandals hit. And, okay—it was pretty amazing. Walking down a wide street lined with towering trees sporting their fall colors was like staring into a movie. The reds, oranges, and yellows mingled together, giving the street a tranquil aura. It was all very poetic. Until a pigeon decided that the top of my head was a great place to defecate. Yeah, even the pigeons here are against me.

The only two things that Paris *didn't* get wrong are the shopping and the food. The former was tragic for my bank account, and my credit card is almost maxed out. But since I'm leaving tomorrow, it's not a big deal.

I'm glad to be heading home, but facing Jeff won't be easy. How am I going to tell him that I'm not interested? He probably believes all those falsehoods they feed us about Paris, which means he expects a positive answer from me. I love my job, and the promotion would be great for my career. But honestly, would anyone willingly live somewhere where the trash hasn't been collected for an entire week?

I mean, come on, people. I know there's a strike going on, but this is *not* okay.

That said, Jeff's disappointment will be nothing compared to my own. I didn't want to make the move at first, but I had high hopes for my new Parisian life. Instead, I was slapped with a reality check. My life is just as dull here in Paris as it is in the US. Turns out, the location has nothing to do with my misery. And it won't get better any time soon, because when I return to Florida, I'm going to have to look for a new place to live.

I pad out of the bathroom after my shower and glimpse the partial view of the Eiffel Tower from my window. It really does sparkle at night, and it's gorgeous. Until you decide to go see it closer, almost get run over by a scooter, and slip on a fallen leaf because the ground is still slick from all the rain. Ask me how I know.

Tonight is my last night in Paris, which also means my last dinner. I get dressed in a new outfit I picked up in La Samaritaine yesterday. Well, "picked up" might not be the right words. I had to fight for it, scouring for hours until I finally found my size, but it was totally worth it. Black flared pants are paired with a white lace top and a beige blazer. Very Parisian chic. Even if they don't wear berets, French women still have a great sense of style. I match the outfit with my beloved black stilettos, and I'm good to go. The place I'm visiting tonight is Cezanne, the Michelin-starred restaurant located right here in the hotel. Perfect, since it's been raining all day.

I saunter into the restaurant parlor, which is elegantly decorated in red velvet with gold trimmings.

"Bonsoir," a tall brunette says with a bright smile.

"*Bonsoir. Jay houn reservation pour houn person, sil vou play.*"

At least I've made some progress with my French since I got here. I wasn't too bad in high school and college, so I had a small base to build on. And honestly, I'm glad I had the chance to practice here. It's kind of like riding a bike. Once you learn a little French, it doesn't really go away.

She wears a puzzled frown at first, then nods. She replies in English. "Oh, yes. What's your name?"

I guess I still have to work on that accent.

"Clark."

She peers at her tablet and taps on the screen. "Right this way, Ms. Clark."

I follow her across the dining room, which is beautifully decorated in the same red and gold pairing. The walls look soft and comfy thanks to the velvet, and the entire space sparkles with gold accents from the chandelier and furniture to the paintings adorning the walls. The muraled ceiling is spectacular, showcasing a choir of angels flying in the clouds. Even if it is a tad old-fashioned, this is the most luxurious-looking restaurant I've visited this week. They're really rocking the Rococo style. A picture of this dining room should be pasted next to the word in the dictionary. Couldn't be any more accurate.

Most of the round tables are empty, but that's not unusual for seven o' clock. I'm always the first to arrive. The French tend to eat around eight p.m.

"Here's your table," the waitress announces, drawing out the chair for me. Once I'm seated, she hands me a menu and leaves me to explore my options.

As with most high gastronomy restaurants in Paris, the only offering is a tasting menu. Seven courses tonight, and they all look promising. Two appetizers, a fish course, a meat course, cheese, and two desserts.

After a few minutes, a tall man in glasses comes to my table with a bottle of water.

"Good 'ivening, madame," he says, pouring me a glass. "Can I offer you an *apéritif*? A glass of champagne, maybe?"

"Sure," I reply with a polite smile.

"'Ave you looked at ze menu? Do you 'ave any questions or allergies?"

"No. I eat everything," I say with a cheeky grin, but he doesn't seem to find my quip very amusing.

He promptly takes my menu. "I will be right back wiz your champagne."

I'm not sure what to expect. I try to avoid doing much research before eating somewhere for the first time. That allows me to be completely unbiased while I sample the food and write my critique later. The suspense also makes me extra excited to dig in. All I know is that this is a Michelin three-star restaurant that recently changed chefs. Philippe Brun, a gastronomy legend in France, has stepped down to pass the reins to his promising son.

The first dish lands on my table quickly, and it's a timid start. The mushroom velouté is dull, desperately missing something to stimulate my taste buds. Next comes the pan-fried foie gras with caramelized butternut squash and pears. It's actually not bad—I've never had warm foie gras before, and I think I prefer it to the cold version—but it's not mind-blowing either. The warm toasted gingerbread they served with it was a nice touch, though. The fish is cooked to perfection, but again, it's nothing to write home about. And when the main dish arrives, I'm not even excited anymore.

I take my first bite, and it's good. Everything is tasty and well-executed, but the dish lacks something. There is no creativity, no "wow" factor. It's a miss for me.

"Would you like some cheese, madame?" my waiter asks, pushing a cart in front of him. Here it is, my favorite moment of every meal I've eaten in Paris. Because if there's one thing every Parisian restaurant does well, it's the cheese trolley.

"Yes, of course," I say, wiping my lips with my napkin.

He settles the trolley in front of my table and opens the lid. Then, he proceeds to tell me the names of all the cheeses, but I barely understand, so I pick the tastiest looking varieties I haven't tried yet.

He lays them all on a rectangular slate, sorting them by eating direction before adding various chutneys and candied fruits around them.

"*Bon appétit.*"

"*Merci.*"

I devour my cheese, glad to find that it doesn't disappoint like the rest of the menu did. Like Paris did. At least there's always cheese to save the day.

Olivier

I wipe my forehead with the back of my arm as I lean against the stainless-steel counter. Another service finished. Another night working like a robot executing orders. Another night feeling like a failure.

"*Ça va*, chef?" my pastry chef asks, throwing a towel over his shoulder.

"*Oui. Je vais aller en salle*," I say, bracing myself. The moment when I tour the room at the end of the night used to be one of my favorite beats of the service. Talking to diners, asking if they enjoyed their night. I always loved it. Not because of the compliments I'd receive, but because it's gratifying to hear that our guests had a good time. That the food we served made them happy for a night. I'm always humbled to talk to my guests. With so many Michelin-starred restaurants in Paris, it's an honor that they choose to dine with us. That's why my team and I always give one hundred percent to make their night special.

But that was before. Now that I work here, the meals I serve aren't really mine. And no matter how much I plead to change that, Jean-Pierre, my boss, doesn't want to hear it. That's the problem with working in palaces—a five star hotel who received the prestigious label—the hotel owns the restaurant. You're just executing the menu. Well, usually the head chef has control over that too, but I haven't earned that right yet. As my boss says, "Classic and safe. No need to change anything or take risks. Just follow your father's recipes."

What he doesn't understand is that when you're a chef, you always need to challenge yourself. You have to constantly evolve, otherwise you die slowly. While that's true for anyone who has a creative brain, it's especially true for a chef. And my motives aren't purely selfish. If we stay stuck in our ways and keep serving our clients the exact same thing, they'll look for greener—and tastier—pastures.

Alas, explaining that to Jean-Pierre, who comes to work wearing the same tie *every day,* is a lost cause. I've tried countless times these past few months, but he always shuts me down. After all, he hired me for my family name, not for my talent or ideas.

Taking a deep breath, I push through the swinging doors to the dining room. The restaurant is packed, but I'm not sure how long that will last. We've gotten some nasty reviews lately, a lot of them from first-timers or occasional guests who wanted to try my cuisine but were disappointed because of how similar it was to my dad's. An issue Jean-Pierre brushed off as soon as I brought it up to him. "Don't worry, Olivier," he said. "Your dad's cuisine is legendary, so this is by no means a bad thing. Plus, we have a lot of returning customers here who have certain expectations."

Straightening my posture, I begin my tour of the room, asking clients how their meal was. Some say they enjoyed it, and some have a few critiques to make, but most bear the same expression. The one that says, "It was good, but nothing spectacular." And I hate that look. I cook to convey emotions, positive ones of course. I want to make people feel something when they eat my food. I wish for them to remember their dinner, remember the taste in their mouths. But once again, I failed miserably.

I'm approaching the last table in the room, and my breath catches in my lungs. Sitting at the table is a beautiful woman. Shoulder-length dark-brown hair, slightly wavy and glossy. But it's her eyes that sparkle the most. Even brighter than the hideous golden fixtures that litter the room. As I draw closer, I try to settle on a color, but I can't decide between brown and green. What surprises me most is that she's eating alone.

"*Bonsoir,*" I say, a genuine smile on my face. "*J'espère que vous avez passé une bonne soirée.*"

"*Bonsoir,*" she says with a cute American accent. "*Merci. C'était bonne, oui. Mais quelques* things *étaient* . . . disappointing.*"

"Oh, I'm sorry the meal didn't meet your expectations," I say, her words all too familiar. "Was there something in particular?"

"Yes," she says, clearly relieved to be speaking English. "I found the first course to be kind of dull. There was no spark or flavor, really. A bit boring, if I can be blunt."

"Please," I say, forcing a tight smile. Usually, I wouldn't worry about criticisms from an American—they don't have the same palate as us—but if even the foreigners aren't enjoying my cuisine, we're barreling straight into the wall.

"The rest was good, but I was expecting a twist on the traditional recipes. It all lacked creativity and passion, in my opinion."

There used to be twists, I say inwardly. Until Jean-Pierre tasted my dishes and told me to go back to the original recipes. "I understand," I say, my tone polite. She seems to know what she's talking about. "Is there anything you liked?"

Her brownish green eyes warm. "I liked the foie gras and the cheese."

Great. Two things I didn't even make.

"Are you here on vacation or for work?" I ask, unable to tear my gaze away from her. I should run, honestly. This situation isn't pleasant by any means. But for some reason, my feet stay firmly planted on the ground. Maybe I'm becoming a masochist. It wouldn't be a surprise, given my disastrous love life and how long I willingly stayed with women who were taking advantage of me.

"Work," she says, smiling for the first time. And damn, that smile is beautiful. The entire room—and my mood—lights up instantly. "It's my last day. Going back to Florida tomorrow." She scratches the back of her neck, averting her eyes. "I came to Paris for a historical tour—I'm an historian—well a researcher for a university."

"And a foodie, obviously."

She nods, her smile widening. "Oh, absolutely. That's why I was thrilled the university sent me here. I got to try so many amazing restaurants."

And mine wasn't one of them, I silently add, looking away. "Well, thank you for dining with us. Enjoy the rest of your trip, and have a safe flight back to Florida," I say as pleasantly as possible.

She blushes slightly. *"Merci."*

As I spin on my heel and march back to the kitchen, I breathe a sigh. Being a chef has never really helped me in the love department, but for one brief second, I imagine how different this conversation could have gone if I'd served her a meal that swept her off her feet. Maybe, I would have been bold enough to ask her out. Maybe, she'd have said yes, and we could have enjoyed a fantastic night in Paris together. But the truth is, I'm a failure, so there will be no late-night romantic escapade for me.

Chapter 3

Olivier

When I pull myself out of bed the next day, I can't help but browse the reviews for Cezanne to see if new ones have been posted. Like I said, I might just be a masochist.

A wave of relief washes over me when I see none, but a pang of disappointment hits too. I was kind of hoping to find a nasty review from a certain American history teacher.

I think I need to get my brain checked out.

Trudging into the shower, I stand under the hot water longer than usual, the scent of my lemongrass and cinnamon body wash warming up my brain. Then, I eat some leftover buns for breakfast before heading out to the farmer's market for some inspiration.

When I get home, my creative juices are flowing, and two hours later, I'm tasting a new and improved version of my dad's famous dish.

I close my eyes and savor the flavors and textures. A smile builds on my lips. This is good. Really good. There's the traditional sauce that makes this dish so special, but the splash of citrus and aromatic herbs bring a fresh twist that tickles the taste buds. This dish is classic enough to please the old generation and satisfy returning customers, but the new additions bring a hint of novelty. Jean-Pierre needs to taste this. When he does, maybe he'll finally understand what I can bring to the table. Literally. And I'll finally have one of my own recipes on the menu.

Placing a portion in a to-go container, I glance at the wall clock. I need to get going if I want to see him before my shift starts.

But, of course, getting to work is an absolute nightmare today. The streets have been congested all week because of the strike. Frankly, I'm surprised the city is still standing at this point. Between the daily demonstrations, groups of young rioters breaking store windows and setting cars on fire, and now the garbage collectors striking, this city has quickly gone from bad to worse.

I make it to work with barely fifteen minutes on the clock. Rushing into the kitchen, I heat up the meal for Jean-Pierre in the microwave. Not ideal, but it'll do.

"Not now, Olivier," Jean-Pierre groans when I run into him in the corridor. His tie is disheveled and his hair messy, like he's been yanking on it all morning. "Today is not the day. Half of the housekeeping staff just went on strike."

"Come on. Just a taste," I beg, holding the dish in front of me. "Please. I think you'll like it. It'll make your day just a little better."

He sighs, setting his pile of documents on a console in the corridor. "Fine."

I give him the plate, and he tries a couple of forkfuls. "What part of 'stick to the original recipe' don't you understand?"

My heart falls. "I did stick to the original recipe. I just added—"

"No adding anything," he fires back, his face reddening. "Please, don't waste any more of my time. Just make sure you follow your dad's recipes to a T."

I nod, swallowing the dry lump in my throat. "Yes, sir."

All I want is a chance to show off my talents, have my own identity, be treated as a chef—not just a cook. But stepping into my father's shoes is a lot harder than I imagined. And I knew it would be plenty hard. My dad has big shoes to fill.

He was a three Michelin star chef for most of his career. He worked right here, in this Parisian landmark, for three decades before I took over. That's the only reason they even considered me for the job.

Though I've been off to a rocky start, I've finally earned the respect of my dad. In fact, I think this is the first time he's ever been proud of me. After I earned my stripes around the globe, he said I was finally seeing reason, working in France again, and in a palace where I belong. It's an incredible opportunity, he reminded me.

And he's right. Working in a palace opens a lot of doors, and it's a great learning experience. The job is rigorous and prestigious, but it's also not as liberating as other venues I've cooked at. There are countless rules and expectations in palaces. Especially when you have my last name.

Jean-Pierre gathers his documents back into a pile. "I knew you'd need a few months to find your footing, but this is taking longer than I thought. Don't forget, Michelin stars are awarded in March, and we don't know if the critics have come yet. If we lose a star—the first in over thirty years—you'll be out of here faster than a hot knife through butter. And good luck finding another establishment that will hire you after that," he adds, his blue eyes icing me out. "Do you understand?"

"Yes, sir," I say with a nod, feeling like a puppet on a string. I wish I could scream at him to make him listen, but that's not how I was raised. And when you work in kitchens all your life, you learn to obey orders.

The truth is, I wouldn't be the only one responsible if we did lose a star. The restaurant has been declining for a while. As we've established, I'm something of a comment lurker, and the slew of bad or average reviews started trickling in last year. Before I even set foot in this kitchen.

My dad is an excellent cook, but he was very much set in his ways. He'd been serving the same menu for over a decade. When he had a health scare last spring, the management suggested that he retire. I was the natural choice to take his place since I had been working there as his second for a few months. He wasn't keen on the idea at first, but he eventually agreed, nudged by the doctors and my mom, who had been dying to spend evenings with her husband and have her weekends back.

So, yeah. There's a lot more on the line than just my reputation—or the restaurant's. It's my father's legacy.

Hazel

"*Your flight has been canceled,*" the email preview on my phone says. When I first read the words, all the blood drained from my face. I must be as white as the meringue I'm currently eating.

I open the email and skim through it. No, no, no. This can't be happening. I was well aware this was a possibility, since the air traffic controllers started striking yesterday, but I assumed my flight had slipped through the cracks since I hadn't received a cancellation notification. Well, here it is now. *Great*. They really like to wait until the last minute, don't they? Well, technically, my flight was supposed to leave in four hours, but still.

I try to call the airline's customer service number, but the line is so busy, it doesn't even let my call through. Reading a couple of articles online, I discover with horror that the strike is expected to continue for one to two weeks. That's a one-week minimum!

I immediately punch in Jeff's number.

"*Bonjour*," he says in his usual cheery voice.

"Hey, Jeff," I grumble, my tone bleak. "Cheery" is not the mood over here. "Bad news. Air and train traffic controllers joined the strike, and I'm stuck for a while—not sure how long. I can't even reach the freaking airline. But if what I read online is true, it'll be one week at least."

"Oh, I see," he mutters. "Well, more time for you to enjoy all the fun Paris has to offer, then. Thank you for sending in your reviews, by the way. I haven't replied yet because we've been swamped this week, but we'll get them edited and posted ASAP. I'll let you know. And since you're stuck there, I'll send a list of new restaurants for you to try, but you'll have to get a table yourself. This extra leg of your trip will give you even more time to make your decision."

A loud snort escapes me. "Oh, my decision is made, Jeff. This city is not what I expected *at all*."

"Is it . . . better?" His voice is tentative.

"No, it's not better," I say louder than I intended, earning me side glances from the people sitting next to me in the café.

"Ah, well." I picture him scratching his head like he always does when someone dares challenge his overly joyous mood. "Maybe a few more days will change your mind."

"Sure," I say, not bothering to hide the sarcasm that leaks into my tone.

"Okay. Well, I'll send over that list in a little bit. Talk to you soon."

I heave out a long breath. "Bye, Jeff."

As expected, talking to Jeff only pumped up my anger meter. Having a bubbly boss is beyond frustrating. Anyway, it's not like he can do anything about my situation. It's not his fault I'm stuck here. I'll just have to go back to the hotel and see if I can extend my st—

Oh, crap.

Calling the *garçon* over, I pay for my meal and hustle back to the hotel as fast as my stilettos allow. And when I arrive, the bad feeling I'd had proves right. The once-chic and airy lobby has lost its grandeur. The golden fixtures and massive flower arrangements are still here, but their opulence is tainted by the dozens of tourists cramped in the space, yelling at the staff or trying to calm their fussy children down.

Yeah. This is going to be a long night.

Chapter 4

Hazel

After standing in line for three hours—yes, you read that right—it's finally my turn to speak to a receptionist. He's doing his best to look polite and cheerful, but I can tell that he wants nothing more than to yell to the clambering crowd that there are no more rooms available. Because there aren't. I've heard him say just that to the people in line before me. But I also heard there was a waiting list, and I want in on it. I've searched online for another room elsewhere in the city, and there is absolutely zero availability in Paris right now. Yes, it sounds unbelievable, but it's true. That's what happens when every tourist is simultaneously stuck here during the high season. I'm also suspecting that my airline *particularly* sucked, having notified me at the very last minute when others might have been informed sooner. It didn't help that my flight was scheduled for eleven-fifty p.m.

"I'd like to be put on the waiting list, please. My name is Hazel Clark, I left room 2805 this morning."

"Of course." He types on his keyboard. "Done," he says. "There is no room available now, but we will call you if one does become available. In the meantime, I would suggest looking into another lodging option or going to the airport where they have set up a camp."

From a palace to an airport floor. The French really are romantics.

"Right." I weigh my options, but I truly don't have a choice. "Could you order me a taxi, please?"

"Sure." He nods, typing again. "Please join the queue over there." He points to the far end of the lobby, where dozens of people are sitting on armchairs or leaning against the carpeted walls, waiting. "The taxi services are a little backed up right now, but it shouldn't be more than a few hours."

"Thank you," I mumble before joining the back of the line. This day just keeps getting better and better.

I recline my back against the wall, standing behind a family of six. The children must all be between three and eight years old, tops, and they're all whining, crying, or yelling at each other.

After being awake for sixteen hours and standing in line forever, I don't even have it in me to be annoyed. Frankly, I feel cranky too, and I wish I could let it out.

"Excuse me," a voice says behind me, catching my attention. Wait, I recognize that voice. When I turn my head, my eyes fall on Olivier Brun, the hotel restaurant's head chef from last night, who's fighting his way through a group of Chinese tourists. Even in my exhausted state, I notice how delicious he looks again today. The guy seems more like a model than a chef. Even if—I must admit—the uniform is what does it for me. He probably lights the kitchen on fire every time he sets foot in it. Seeing him again, I think I could forgive the average-tasting meal I endured yesterday. Maybe that's why he tours the dining room at the end of the service. To blind diners with his good looks so they forget all about the lackluster meal. *Focus, Hazel*. I don't get dazzled that easily. That's the difference between regular people and professionals.

He must sense my gaze, because when he wheels around, he looks straight at me. And because I've apparently grown up in the last two minutes from a cranky toddler to a hormonal teenager, my heart leaps in my chest, and I snap my head away.

"Hello, there." His deep timbre forces me to meet his eyes again. And holy moly is he hot. Sharp jaw, medium-length wavy brown hair with a stylish brushup, green eyes, and a dimpled smile that's to die for. He's in excellent shape too. Those strong arms must be handy when mixing those heavy sauces and batters.

"Oh, hi," I say, pulling myself into focus. I attempt to arrange my hair, but I don't need a mirror to tell me I'm failing miserably. "I didn't see you there." *Really, Hazel?*

The corner of his mouth twitches into a smile, exposing that deadly dimple. "Is everything okay? Did you manage to get a room?" he asks with a subtle French accent.

I sigh. "No. But I'm waiting on a taxi for the airport. I think. So, that's something."

His eyebrows scrunch together. "So, your flight hasn't been canceled?"

"Oh, yes, it is very much canceled. Dead on the ground. *Not* flying. But they have mattresses set up over there. Those are on the ground too, I believe." Gosh, why am I babbling? This is starting to get ridiculous. Yes, this man is as hot as a pizza oven, but that's no reason to lose my cool.

He chuckles lightly, and I almost melt into a puddle on the floor. It must be because I'm tired. Men don't have that effect on me. *Ever.*

Sure, I get attracted to guys like the next girl, but this is different. And since I'm not into French men—and anyway, he's not even wearing a beret—that can't be the case. My lack of sleep is the only plausible answer.

"I see. Well, this might be kind of inappropriate," he says, his tender gaze twisting my gut, "but I do have an extra bedroom if you need a place to crash for a few days."

"No thanks," I blurt out louder than intended. No, going to this gorgeous specimen's house is not a good idea. And not because I'm dying to try out the military sleeping bag they probably have set up at the airport. It's because the last thing I need is to fall for a French guy—who, may

I remind you, is not even wearing a beret—when I already hate this city. If I fall for him, I'll be stuck here for good, and I'll end up on the side of the road, like all the forgotten trash, when he eventually throws me away.

He frowns. "*Comme vous voulez.* I was just offering. Have a nice evening, then."

Evening? It's one a.m. What is he talking about? This man is clearly as worn out as I am. "Yeah, you too."

What is wrong with me? Refusing a bed, and probably an excellent breakfast, from this very fine gentleman. I should have said thank you and followed him out the door. Instead, I chose a sleeping bag that probably smells like feet as I cram up against a thousand roomies. Plus, just because I have the hots for this guy doesn't mean he's even remotely interested in me. That wasn't the vibe I got from his offer at all. He was just being friendly because I was a restaurant guest. Nothing more. Besides, I'm sure he already has a wife or a girlfriend or whatever. And even if he doesn't, why would he even find me attractive right now when I look like a hag? Even on my best day, I can't compete with the gorgeous women that walk the streets here.

Accepting his offer would have been the sane thing to do. He wasn't even flirting with me. Gosh, I really am a lost cause. I've been burned by men so badly, I can't even recognize a kind gesture from a nice guy when I see one. And he clearly is a nice guy. I didn't hold back when I critiqued his cuisine yesterday, yet here he was, offering me some much-needed help. My skin itches at the thought, and guilt washes over me. This is why we're not supposed to create links with chefs we're evaluating. It muddies the water and makes you feel like crap afterwards. Yet here I am, considering his offer. Desperate times call for desperate measures, right?

I run outside—well, "run" is a big word. I don't run. I *speed-walk* in my stilettos, dragging my large suitcase behind me. As I hustle down the street, I catch sight of him as he's about to turn the corner.

"Olivier," I yell. "Olivier." Obviously, I'm not shouting loud enough, because he doesn't hear me. It might be the middle of the night, but there are a lot of people out on the street. In addition to everyone being stuck here against their will, it's Friday night. I continue chasing him down, trying my best to avoid dog droppings and wet leaves—learned my lesson—while zig-zagging between angry tourists and groups of drunken youngsters smoking cigarettes. Forget sleeping in a real bed tonight. I'll be lucky if I get out of here alive.

I'm at the corner now, but I can't keep up my pace. This street is less crowded, so I try my luck again. "Olivier!" I yell at the top of my lungs, and it does the trick. He turns around, and a smile springs to his face when he sees me. Granted, I must look like a crazy person right now.

Catching my breath, I shuffle toward him, and he meets me halfway.

"I changed my mind," I gasp, hands on my knees. "If you're still offering your bed, I'll take it."

He arches an eyebrow at the exact same moment I realize what I just said.

"No! Sorry," I stammer, my face now effectively on fire. "Not what I meant. I—"

"*Pas de problème*," he says with a coy smile. "You must be tired. Let's go."

My shoulders slump with relief that he's still keen on letting me crash despite the level of crazy I just showcased. *"Merci*. It's been a long day."

He yawns while stretching his arms over his head. "Yes, it has. Here, let me help you with that."

Taking the handle of my rolling suitcase, he starts dragging it down the sidewalk. "Geez. What are you carrying in there? A dead body?"

That makes me smile. Not an easy task given my current state, I assure you. "Maybe."

He chuckles. "Well, in that case, I won't ask any more questions. I don't want to be an accessory to murder."

My smile widens. "Good thinking."

He shakes his head as he begins walking again, and I follow suit. After a few steps, his head snaps toward me.

"You were joking, right?"

A loud laugh bubbles from my chest. "Believe me, the only thing I'm guilty of is my inability to resist Paris' incredible shopping."

He dramatically sweeps his forehead with the back of his hand. "Phew. *Dieu Merci.* I thought so, but it doesn't hurt to make sure. Your country is well known for serial killers, after all."

I strangle a laugh. "Right. Well, the only thing I killed this week was my credit card limit."

"Perfectly acceptable," he jokes as we stroll into a parking lot, and I almost sigh with relief. I was praying we wouldn't have to take the metro.

"Plus," I add, "if there's one thing I learned this week, it's that most clichés are completely off base."

He shoots me a curious look. "I was referring to statistics, but sure, let's go with 'cliché.' It'll help me sleep tonight. Especially since I don't even know your name."

I nudge him with my elbow, and he just chuckles. "It's Hazel, by the way."

"Hazel, *enchanté*," he says, and his voice sends warm tingles coursing through my body. The way he says my name—now that's something else. It's as if the syllables glide on his tongue and roll off his lips. Like my name is coated with sugar and completely irresistible.

"Here's my car," he says, pointing to a black compact vehicle. "Let's go home."

Oui, monsieur.

Chapter 5

Olivier

When I wake up, my eyelids are heavy, like I've just fallen asleep. Or maybe I haven't slept at all. In my defense, my night did take an unexpected turn—to say the least—and I was too electrified to close an eye. Possibly because of the spunky American historian sleeping next door, and the fact that even after running down the street in heels at one in the morning, she looked as breathtaking as the first time I saw her. But let's not go there. I'm just helping her out. Nothing more. When I saw her in the lobby, I couldn't leave without offering my spare room. Not as a thank you, because she hated my food, nor to make up for the uninspired meal. But because she looked so defeated and alone, and the sight made my heart break. The offer just came out naturally. I didn't overthink it.

Glancing at the wall clock, I realize it's already noon. Looks like I did manage to sleep a little after all. I yank the covers off and hop out of bed. My stomach is gurgling now, begging for breakfast. Sliding on a pair of pants, I shuffle into the living room. The house is quiet, so I assume Hazel is still sleeping.

My place is small, but for Paris' suburbs, it's not bad. There's a small garden in the back and a single-car driveway. It's a quaint bungalow with two bedrooms, a bathroom, a laundry room, and a large living area that opens into the best corner of the house—the kitchen. I chose every inch of it when I first moved into this house. From the marble countertops to the appliances, nothing has been decided lightly. This is, after all, the most important room of a household. At least, it is for me, being the room where I spend most of my time.

In honor of my American guest, I settle on cinnamon pancakes. Grabbing my utensils and ingredients as silently as possible, I get to work, now fully awake and pumped for the day.

When I'm done with the batter, I let it rest to ensure maximum fluffiness. Then, I check the fridge and realize I don't have maple syrup—a crime, I know, given it's fall. Placing both hands on the counter, I brainstorm a solution. Either I wait an hour and go to the store, or I try to make something up on the spot. I open my fridge again and survey what I'm working with. Butter, right. That will do. I could just let it melt on top and then sprinkle some powdered sugar and cinnamon over it. Or, I could melt the butter in a pan, then add powdered sugar, cream cheese, milk, and vanilla to make a rich cinnamon-roll-like glaze. My mouth starts to water. Looks like we have a winner.

I've just started frying the pancakes when Hazel steps out of my guest room wearing a dark satin pajama set that complements her curvy figure well.

"Morning," she mumbles, rubbing her eyes.

"*Bonjour*. Sorry if I woke you. I was starving."

"Oh, no. You didn't wake me. For some reason, my brain just decided it was acceptable to switch itself on full-throttle after only six hours of sleep."

I chuckle, flipping the pancakes in the oversized pan.

"That smells amazing," she says, coming closer and breathing in deeply. "Is that cinnamon?"

"Yes. Cinnamon pancakes. I hope you'll like them. It's not one of our country's specialties, but I always prefer pancakes over crêpes for breakfast. They're more filling."

"Well, I have a thing for crêpes, so I don't know if I can agree with that judgment. But that's probably because pancakes are so common for me," she says with a small smile. "Can I?" She glances toward the high stool behind the central island.

I wave my spatula. "Of course. Sorry. Where are my manners? Like I told you last night, make yourself comfortable, and feel free to use any furniture."

"Thanks. And I'd say your manners are pretty polished. You're cooking me breakfast, after all," she says, her eyes teasing with laughter. "Some of that is for me, right?"

I nod, a grin escaping. "Yes, of course."

"Looks like I'm the one with bad manners. I should be offering my help. And if you were anyone else, I would, but I wouldn't dare touch anything in a chef's kitchen."

That makes me laugh. "Why not? We don't bite."

"I'm sure you have your methods and habits, and I wouldn't want to mess it all up for you."

"I guess you're right, but that's not just a chef thing. It's a human thing. I love cooking with company, actually, but please stay seated," I say with a smile when I see she's about to stand up. "Because I'm almost done, and the fun part, otherwise known as the eating part, is about to start. Can I offer you some coffee?"

"Please."

I grab two mugs from the cabinet and fill them with the filtered coffee I started earlier.

"Thank you," she says as I place the mug in front of her. "It's really beautiful out here," she adds, gazing out the window. "I love how you can really see the seasons in Paris. One glance outside, and you can tell it's fall."

I follow her gaze. I must admit, today is particularly beautiful. The glow of the sun reflects on the trees bursting with color. It's almost like there's an orange and yellow filter in the glass of the window.

"It's not like that where you live?"

She snorts, turning her eyes back to me. "Florida has two seasons—wet and dry. Trees do change colors in the north, but it's super quick and definitely not as dramatic as it is here."

Frankly, I never paid too much attention to the fall foliage. I love nature, but I'm so caught up in my work and the day-to-day hustle, I forget to appreciate the simple things. "You do have warmer weather in Florida, though. In a few weeks, it's going to get really cold here. Trust me."

She wraps her hands around her coffee mug. "I guess you're right."

I clasp my hands together. "And now, the food."

"Yes," she chirps, her eyes sparkling as I serve her a plate of three—hopefully fluffy and delicious—pancakes.

"I made a sauce, but I don't know if you'll like it. So try it first, okay?" I place a small porcelain jar of the creamy sauce next to her.

"Fancy," she says, lifting the jar and checking it out. She holds it to her nose and inhales. "What is it? It smells familiar."

"Guess," I say with a smile, serving myself some pancakes.

She places a finger on her lips and lifts her eyes to mine. "Hmm. The only thing I can make out is vanilla?"

I nod. "Try it."

She pours some of the glaze into a spoon and studies it before bringing it to her lips.

"Milk and butter?" she proposes, her forehead wrinkled in thought. "But I'm missing something."

"Yes. But you're getting warmer," I tease, drizzling some of the sauce on my pancakes.

"I can't put my finger on it, but it's something I've eaten before, for sure. It kind of reminds me of the glaze on top of . . . Yes! That's it. It's cinnamon roll glaze. What's the last ingredient, though?"

My smile widens, hurting my cheeks. "You're good. It's cream cheese."

She nods. "Makes sense."

"Now, try it."

She shakes her head. "Right."

I freeze as she brings a mouthful of pancakes drenched in sauce to her lips, fork in one hand, knife in the other. Holding my breath, I watch her like I'm at a cooking competition, and she's the jury.

"Delicious," she gushes. At her verdict, my entire body relaxes. Finally, she likes some of my cooking.

A silence falls between us, but it's not uncomfortable. After a few minutes, we both finish our plates.

"Thank you again, so much, for letting me crash here," she says, tucking a strand of brunette hair behind her ear. "I promise I'll be out of here as soon as possible."

"So, my cooking still didn't convince you, huh?" I shake my head, closing my eyes. "Tough crowd."

Her face lights up. "Are you kidding? This was the most delicious breakfast I've eaten in—well, ever," she says, her compliment going straight to my heart. "I just don't want to impose, that's all. And by the way, I did like your cooking before. At the restaurant."

"No, you're not imposing. I offered." I cast her a smile. "And yes, that's exactly what I'm talking about. Like is not *love,* and that's what I always aim for when I cook for someone. But alas, you can't win every time. You were right, though, the other night. It wasn't a proper display of my skills. I should have done better."

She blushes. "I'm sorry if I offended you or your cooking in any—"

"Don't. It's part of the job. You can't please everyone. And like I said, it definitely wasn't my best night. Which is why you *must* stay here a bit longer. So I can redeem myself and show you what I can do," I add with a wink.

Biting her lip, she rips out a laugh.

I frown, looking away. "Gosh, that sounded incredibly arrogant, didn't it?"

She nods, unable to speak through her laughter.

"Well, what do you know? Some clichés might be true after all," I joke. "It is something people say, right? That the French are arrogant."

"I think I've heard that once or twice," she says between giggles. "But you're not, I can already tell. There's always an exception to the rule."

I chuckle. "Thank goodness. I wouldn't want to change your views on clichés and false expectations. Paris didn't live up to the hype, huh?"

She winces. "You could say that. I came here hoping to fall in love with this old, romantic city and accept a job here. Instead, I've never missed home so much."

I wince. "Ouch. That bad?"

"I don't mean any disrespect," she utters, wringing her hands. "It just didn't do the trick for me."

"I get it. Foreigners have such a romanticized view of Paris, and France in general, that it can be quite a shock when they get here. Especially now, with the strike going on."

"Yeah . . . It's just super dirty everywhere, and people aren't very nice here. Everyone smokes, and there's a lot of pollution. Plus, it rains. All. The. Time. Coming from Florida, I'm used to warmer weather and—oh my goodness. Am I just being the brattiest American ever? That's another cliché, right?"

Now it's my turn to laugh. "You're fine. I was about to ask anyways. What were you expecting coming in?"

She shrugs. "Great food, fantastic shopping, a romantic atmosphere with accordions playing at every corner, and nice people wearing berets and holding baguettes?"

"Like every American movie set in France, basically." I laugh hard, and she joins me.

"Obviously, I was way off. Well, the shopping was great but more expensive than I thought. And finding my size hasn't always been easy. But the food was the highlight of my trip. Just one tiny disappointment—I didn't eat one single snail or frog leg."

"Because those aren't everyday dishes for us," I say with a chuckle. "I might eat snails once or twice a year, tops—usually around Christmastime. As for frog legs, I don't even remember the last time I had them. A few years ago, maybe. I know we're famous for those because they're weird dishes, but they're really not a part of our routine."

She sighs. "That sucks. I was really hoping to try some."

"I'll see what I can do," I say with a wink, already unraveling a recipe in my head.

"And here you told me you weren't a good host. I beg to differ."

My heart bounces in my chest, but I ignore the feeling and laugh politely instead.

"Seriously, though." Her warm eyes settle on me. "Thank you. If there's anything I can do to repay you, let me know."

"No worries," I say with a wave of my hand.

She gets up. "Let me at least clean this up for you."

"Oh no, you don't have to."

"I want to. Please, it's the least I can do," she says with a tone that leaves no room for argument.

"I wash, you dry?" I suggest.

She nods. "Sure."

We head over to the sink and get to work on the dishes, chatting about the different restaurants she's tried during her week here. I'm impressed with the prestigious tables she's dined at. I had the feeling she knew what she was talking about the other night at the restaurant, and that confirms my suspicions. This girl is no rookie when it comes to high gastronomy, and I can only agree with the praise she's showering on my colleagues.

The way she talks about food is exceedingly attractive. I feel her passion as she describes the flavors and textures of the dishes she tried, but my blood also simmers with jealousy. This is why I cook, to make people feel something. And I know I didn't elicit the same emotions my colleagues did. Something has to be done about this. *Tout de suite.*

Chapter 6

Olivier

Hazel is taking a shower, so I turn on the TV to watch the news. Paris erupted in chaos last night, the worst riot since the strike started. An entire building was set on fire—right in the middle of the city. I'm racking my brain to guess the outcome of this strike, but no compromise seems good enough to end it. Only a change of government would work at this point, but our president is way too arrogant for that. Even if the cliché isn't true for every French citizen, it is in this case.

My phone vibrates next to me on the couch, and my mom's face flashes on the screen.

"*Salut, Maman*," I say, picking up.

"*Mon chéri*, how are you?" she asks, not hiding the concern in her voice. "Did you get home safely? It was mayhem last night."

"I'm fine, *Maman*. Don't worry about me. How about you?"

"Oh, I can't complain. Your father and I stayed in and watched *Danse Avec Les Stars*."

I suppress a laugh. Mom's typical Friday night routine. Dad must have been *thrilled*. The change of pace is good for him, though. After his health scare, he's safer at home in front of the TV.

"Are you working tonight?" she asks.

"Of course, Mom. It's Saturday, the biggest night of the week. But don't worry, I'll be there for your birthday tomorrow." The restaurant closes every week from Sunday to Tuesday, thankfully. "Then, I have a vacation week coming up," I add.

"*Ah, oui*. For the fall festival! The girls will be thrilled. Don't work too hard though, *mon chéri*. Vacation is a time to relax too."

I roll my eyes. "I will, Mom."

"Well, anyway," she coos in that scheming tone I don't like. At all. "The party tomorrow is the reason I called. I ran into Justine Gardinet at the store yesterday, and—"

"Mom," I warn, sensing full well where this is going. My mom's only goal in life is to meddle with the lives of her sons and fix us up with girls. Now that she got my younger brother set up and married with two kids, her entire focus is on me. But I'm not interested. After the way my last relationship ended, I'm perfectly happy staying single for a while.

"She's a nice girl. You were in high school together."

A breath hisses through my teeth. "Yes, I remember, *Maman*." In particular, I recall the unibrow she sported and the creepy cemetery she built for dead insects—ones that I'm pretty sure *she* killed.

"Well," she insists with that dramatic tone again. "She would love to reconnect. I'm pretty sure she has a crush on you. Isn't that wonderful?"

I stay quiet.

"*Sooo*, I invited her over tomorrow."

"You did what?" I scream into the phone. Has she lost her mind?

"No need to yell, son. You'll thank me later. She's a really sweet girl, and she's available. Having grown up in a military family, she understands the demands of your job, and I'm sure you'll hit it off."

Blood threatens to pulse out of my temples. "No. Absolutely not. Do we need to have that talk again, *Maman?* The one we had a few weeks ago when I told you I didn't need your help to meet girls?"

"Well, I'd argue you do, since you're still single. I know men stay attractive longer than women, but you're not getting any younger, *mon chéri.*"

"I'm only twenty-nine, Mom!"

"Exactly. Thirty is right around the corner."

I huff. "It doesn't matter. I'm not ready to date again," I declare.

"Olivier, what Emeline did to you was hurtful, but not every girl is like that, I promise. You will find someone who—"

"Stop it, *maman*," I say with a controlled tone, even as my body tenses. I don't need the reminder. "Call her right now and cancel."

"I will do no such thing," she says with finality. "It's my birthday, after all. Don't you want to make me happy? I thought you'd be a little nicer with your mother on her birthday. This is not how I raised you."

Merde. Not the mom guilt. She always gets me with that. I draw a long, steady breath, almost ready to surrender. Then, a loud bang echoes from the bathroom, followed by a string of cursing, and a lightbulb flickers on in my head.

"I met someone," I blurt. "That's why I don't want you to set me up."

"Oh! Really?" Her delight is palpable through the phone. "Well, that changes everything. Why didn't you say something sooner, boy?" she scolds with a reproaching tone. If we were in the same room, I know she would have swatted my hand, just like when I was a kid. "Okay, I'll cancel."

Relief swooshes the air from my lungs. "*Merci.*"

"All right. I've got to go now, but I'll see you tomorrow. I can't wait to meet this lovely lady. What's her name?"

"What—*non, maman.* I can't bring her. It's still new. I don't want to scare her off."

"Olivier," she says, channeling her mom voice again. "Are you lying to me?"

I swallow hard. "Of course not."

She tuts. "You should be ashamed of yourself." Her tone seems more hurt than disappointed, and I hate it.

"I'm not lying, *maman*." I swear, I sound just like a teenager. "She's real. She's American, and her name is Hazel."

"*Super*. Bring her, then. We're not monsters, Olivier. We're your family."

"*Maman* . . ." I groan.

"Or I can call Justine to confirm for tomorrow."

Crap. She's really not playing around. I release a defeated sigh. "Fine. We'll be there at twelve."

"*Parfait. À demain.*"

"Bye, *maman*."

I fall back against the couch, closing my eyes and trying to make sense of what just happened. Right then, Hazel strides out of the bathroom in a pair of dark-gray yoga pants and a white sweater, a towel tied around her hair.

I guess it's my turn to come clean now.

"It's really crazy out there," she says, her eyes glued to the muted TV as she sits down next to me.

Not as crazy as what I'm about to tell you, I silently say, which doesn't exactly help with my nerves. How do you even bring up something like this? Just spring it on her?

"How long do you think it'll go on?" she asks, a frown creasing her lips.

I return my focus to the screen. "Honestly, I don't know. The whole thing was long overdue. The country has been boiling over for a while."

"That means I'm going to be stuck here forever," she groans, shaking her head. It's followed by a small laugh, but the desolate look on her face tells me she's only half joking. Well, if she already feels trapped, she's really in for a trip when I announce to her what I just told my mom.

"So, um," I say, shifting on the couch. "When you said you'd do anything to repay my hospitality earlier, did you really mean it?"

She turns toward me. "Absolutely! Shoot."

"Before you agree, hold that thought. You might not be so inclined when you hear what I have to say."

"Oh, gosh, is it creepy? Are you into weird fetishes?" she says, scooting a few inches away, but she's still wearing an amused expression.

At least she doesn't actually think I'm a psycho with weird fetishes, so there's that. She'll only think I'm a complete lunatic.

There's no right way to say this, because nothing about it is right. So I just go with my gut instinct and let the words tumble out. "My mom's birthday is tomorrow, and I told her we were dating."

Her hazel eyes widen, showing off more shades of green and brown than I ever thought possible. Forest green, espresso brown, emerald, honey. I could admire them for hours, but my trance is broken when she swats me just like my mom would. "You did what?"

Darn it. She probably has a boyfriend or a husband. Of course she does. She's stunning, and she's here alone on a work trip, not a vacation.

"I know," I say, shaking my head. "I'm sorry. She wanted to set me up with someone, and it just slipped. It was dumb. You know what? Never mind. I'll call her again and admit that I lied. Frankly, I don't know what's gotten into me. The prospect of yet another arranged date messed with my brain," I say, forcing a chuckle.

I grab my phone, once more feeling like a teenager.

Hazel sighs, her features softening. "I know what it's like to have an overbearing mom with a passion for sticking her nose in your love life," she says with a small laugh. Then, she pauses, looking up at the ceiling. My brain must clearly be going haywire because it seems to me like she's actually considering it.

After a moment, she brings her eyes back to me, and to my utmost surprise, she says, "Okay. I'll do it."

My eyes bulge like two marbles. "Wh-What?"

She gives a firm nod. "I'll be your fake girlfriend for your mom's birthday tomorrow."

I do a double take. "Seriously? You will?"

"I did say I'd do anything to repay your kindness, and while it's not what I had in mind, it matches my skill set—I think. My ex-boyfriends might beg to differ, but you didn't say anything about being a *good* girlfriend. Anyway, you're the one who offered, so no backsies—I'll do it."

My mouth falls open. I had a feeling this girl was different, but this exceeds all my expectations. Not that I thought I'd ever find myself in need of a fake girlfriend, but hey, there's a first for everything.

"Okay," I stammer, still trying to wrap my head around what just happened. "Thank you, I guess. Forgive me, I don't know the protocol here."

She laughs hard, and my heart rattles in my chest at the enchanting sound. "You're welcome. So, what do you have planned for today?"

"Work," I say, offering a lopsided smile. "One of the *many* reasons why I don't have a *real* girlfriend to accompany me tomorrow. I work from two p.m. to one a.m. four days a week." Not that I would want a girlfriend anyway. Finding love is the last thing I need right now.

"I get it. Cooking is your passion, right? So, I'm guessing it doesn't even feel like work."

"Yes, you're right. Most of the time, at least." I avert my eyes for a second. "Anyway, I'd better hop in the shower and get ready. Make yourself at home, and feel free to cook or order something to eat for tonight. Or, if you want to go out, I can recommend a few places. I could even drive you on my way to work."

"I think I'll stay in, if that's okay," she says, lifting her eyes to me. "I'll fix myself something to eat later. I'll have to do some work on my laptop since I'm stuck here and everything."

That might be a safer option, I realize. Saturday night is always the craziest night of the week. "Right, the university research."

"Right," she repeats, looking away.

"What are you working on, by the way? I didn't even ask."

"Oh," she says, her eyes fixing on the floor. "Just boring stuff. I wouldn't want to make you late for work. History—especially French history—always takes a while to discuss," she says with a nervous laugh.

"Right." I nod. "Well, I'll go get ready for work, then."

As I brush past her toward the bathroom, I breathe in a subtle mix of warm amber, lemongrass, and cinnamon. My shower gel. She probably used it. Never before has the scent smelled so amazing, attractive, and—dare I say it—*sexy* to me.

That's when I realize how deep in the *merde* I am. Fake dating Hazel might not be such a brilliant idea after all.

Chapter 7

Hazel

I *had* to say yes to Olivier's crazy ploy to please his mom. I know what it's like to have a meddling mother. My heart aches at the thought, as if I've been punched in the chest. Unfortunately, mine is no longer here to interfere with my non-existent love life, and I've missed her every single day these past three years. So, yeah, as crazy as his offer is, I accepted. As much a thank you for his generous hospitality as an homage to my mom. I know she'd be proud.

Plus, I admit I'm a tiny bit curious to meet the legendary Philippe Brun in the flesh. Even if I'm meeting him as his son's fake date.

Oh no! The review. I had this sinking feeling since yesterday, and now I know what's been pricking at my brain. Crap. I need to email Jeff and see if he can hold the article. I grab my phone and start typing, then pause. Wait. What am I doing? I can't ask him to do that. My job was to eat at Olivier's restaurant and write a review based on the meal I had. And it wasn't glorious.

The thing is, I'd give him a five-star review on this morning's breakfast, but the meal I ate at the restaurant paled in comparison. I didn't sense any personality or firm direction in the dishes I tasted. They had no soul, and that makes me even more curious about Olivier. Because from what I'm seeing of the guy, he definitely has one.

Which is why it sucks having to lie to him about my job. When I first met him, I had no choice. Food critics never disclose who they are. But now, it definitely feels sketchy to keep it from him. I contemplate coming clean but decide against it. That would make things weird and awkward between us. He'd know I came to his restaurant to evaluate him and that I didn't approve. And the last thing I want to do is hurt his feelings, especially after a single bad meal when the guy is extremely generous and kind.

That said, I really need to do some research on French history. I almost liquefied on the spot when he asked about my job. Why on earth did I choose that as a cover? I sucked at history when I was in school. I could never remember dates, and I kept messing the names up.

No. The only right thing to do is shut up about my work and return the favor tomorrow. Oh my goodness. Yep. I definitely can't disclose my real job when I'm meeting his family as his *girlfriend*. Especially since his dad is a gastronomy legend here in France. Let's not fill up that awkwardness gauge we have going on. It's plenty uncomfortable already.

Anyway, it doesn't matter. In a few days, I'll be out of here, and our time together will be just a funny anecdote he'll share with his grandkids over *coq au vin*.

My heart pinches at the thought, but I swat the air of melancholy away as I lock my phone. But the screen lights up again, and Ivy's face pops up.

"Hey!" I say, smiling into the phone camera when I see the gorgeous face of my baby sister. She's wearing her work scrubs, and the medical equipment and white walls behind her tell me she's at the hospital.

"Sis, how are you?" She wears a mischievous grin. "Still alive, I see."

I already filled her in on my new host and his statistics about Americans via text last night. To which she replied that only creeps and actual serial killers know those numbers.

I give her a pointed look. "You couldn't have been that worried, since you waited until your lunch break to check up on me."

She waves a hand in dismissal. "I saw your last text when I got up, but I was already late for my shift. Anyway, how's it going? Does he have an amazing apartment? Are you finally getting the unobstructed view of the Eiffel Tower you deserve? That suite in your palace was a little disappointing in that regard."

I bubble out a laugh. I was fine with the partial view, but Ivy is still not over it.

"Nope. It's a house in the suburbs, actually, but it's very nice," I muse while looking around, impressed by how well kept his place is. "You'd never guess a single guy lives here. I'll give you a tour." Flipping the camera around, I take her through the small townhouse. The front door opens to a half-corridor with a bathroom and two bedrooms. On the other side is the spacious living area featuring a dining nook at the far end, a sofa facing a flat-screen TV, and the impressive marble kitchen and bar, which take up half of the space.

"Whoa, that kitchen is spectacular," she says. I turn the camera back around after finishing the tour.

"It really is! And he made me cinnamon pancakes drizzled with cinnamon-roll glaze this morning," I say, my mouth watering at the memory. "Delicious."

"Oh, yeah. You're living your best life, aren't you?"

I roll my eyes at her. "I wouldn't say that. I'm stuck here, and I'd much rather be home, but I'll admit it could be worse. It sure beats airport floors and assembly-line food, that's for sure."

"How long do you think you'll be stuck there?"

I shake my head, blowing out a breath. "It's pretty bad. Every day, another profession seems to go on strike. Hopefully, the debacle will become too big for the government to ignore, and they'll give the people what they want."

"Yeah. The French and their strikes," she jokes. "So, what are you going to do while you're there?"

"Well, I guess I'll work on my articles. Also, Jeff sent me a list of new restaurants to try if I can score a table. They're all booked up online, but I'll try calling in a bit. Oh, and tomorrow, I'm going to Olivier's mom's birthday party."

"You *what*?" she screams. The image shakes so bad, I can barely see her anymore.

"Sorry," her voice peeps, sounding distant. "Dropped the phone."

Her face pops back on the screen. "Did you just say you're going to the Frenchie's mom's birthday dinner?"

My cheeks catch fire. "Well, it's lunch actually, but yes."

Her face twists in confusion. "Why?"

"To thank him for his hospitality and—"

"You're lying," she says. Now she's the one giving me a pointed look, which reminds me so much of our mom's.

"I'm not lying." I wince. "Well, maybe a little. He asked me to pretend to be his date tomorrow. His mother is apparently very much like Mom was, always meddling in his business, trying to marry him off. He doesn't want to endure another arranged date, so he asked for my help. And, as a thank you for his generosity, I agreed."

"So, in other words, you're his beard."

"What! No. At least, I don't think so. He's not gay. No way." I glance around, trying to find the answer. Yes, this house is suspiciously well kept, but everything about Olivier screams virility. From the way his huge biceps stretch his sweaters to the beard on his sharp jaw. Then, there's the intoxicating smell he leaves in his wake and the way he carries himself with confidence.

I fan myself with my hand.

"Okay, if you say so. I mean, even if he is gay, who cares? He has every right to be his authentic self."

"Yes," I blurt a little too loudly. "For sure. Totally." I flash a big smile, pretending I don't care about Olivier's sexual orientation while the heat spreading through my neck tells me I very much do. What's wrong with me? "But no, I'm sure he's not," I say, my brain unfogging. "He mentioned not 'having a girlfriend,' so . . ."

"Okay." She taps a finger on her lips. "Is he super repulsive or something?"

"Ivy!"

"What? Aren't you curious why he's single and in such desperate need of a fake date? If he's not gay and he's good looking, that's kind of sketchy. Especially considering he's a chef! They are like gods over there." A frown clouds her features. "Maybe we ruled out the serial killer thing prematurely."

I shake my head. "There are plenty of reasons why someone would be single. Look at me. Not gay, not a troll—at least I don't think I am—and I haven't killed anyone in a while, so . . ."

"But you're not asking a guy you just met to be your fake date, are you?"

"Well, when he brought it up, I was on board with it so that's something. And he said one of the reasons he's not dating is because his job takes up most of his time."

She sighs. "Well, I hope you have at least set some solid rules in place."

Now, it's my turn to frown. "Rules?"

Her eyes stretch almost as wide as her mouth. "Yes, rules, Haze. Duh! It's the first thing you should have established. The basic building blocks of every healthy fake relationship."

I scratch my neck. "Right. I didn't know you were such an expert."

"Don't you watch romcoms?" she asks, as if this stuff is common knowledge.

I shrug. "Why would I? My life *is* one."

"Oh, really? 'Cause you're the cheery girl with a high-powered job who's meeting a handsome billionaire in an elevator?"

"Nope. I'm the one who cries in front of the TV eating ice cream straight from the carton after a bad breakup. Doesn't that count? Bridget Jones is a romcom, right?"

"I guess so," she relents with a chuckle.

"Well, there you go. I can count the number of times that has happened in the last year alone on both hands. That's embarrassing."

"Exactly. That's why you need those rules."

"Fine," I say, sitting down on the kitchen stool. "What kind of rules are we talking? No intercourse, I'm guessing, right?"

"Hazel!" Ivy squeals again.

I blink a few times, suddenly feeling dizzy. "What? Is that not right? How could it be a healthy fake relationship if we—"

"Of course, no intercourse!" she cuts in. "Oh my gosh, it's a good thing I called you. I need to give you a crash course on this fake dating thing, stat."

Chapter 8

Hazel

I haven't seen Olivier since last night, but I heard him come home at around two a.m. It's after nine, and I've already showered, once again using his incredible cinnamon body wash. Even if it smells a bit masculine, it's delectable. I do have some of my travel-size shower foam left, but I couldn't resist.

When I exit the bathroom, I'm surprised to find Olivier out of his room and eating breakfast at the kitchen bar. A large mug of coffee sits in front of him, and he's dipping a slice of bread in it before bringing it to his mouth. And trust me, I never thought I'd say this, but the way the soaked-up bread melts against his lips, wetting the corner, is unbelievably sexy. It must be a French thing. No one in the States ever looks hot while eating a slice of bread.

He notices my presence and does a double take, probably wondering why I'm staring at him eating breakfast. *"Bonjour!* Please, sit. There's coffee in the pot."

"Hey, thanks." I manage to get my feet moving and pour myself some coffee. Hopefully, the caffeine boost will clear my mind.

As I sit down across from Olivier, I notice the jar of Nutella on the table. Sure enough, there's a generous layer of chocolate hazelnut spread slathered on his bread.

"I figured you'd stay far away from that stuff," I say, glancing at the jar, "being a chef. Fight the rise of processed food and all that." I chuckle, then force myself to take a sip of my tongue-burning coffee before I attempt to make another joke this early in the morning.

My little quip still makes him smile, and I tear my eyes away. "You and your brain full of clichés," he laments, shaking his head.

I choke out a laugh.

Leaning over the bar, he says, "I'll let you in on a little secret. We. Even. Eat. Fast. Food."

A gasp bursts out of me, and I cover my mouth. "You don't!"

He waggles his eyebrows. "Oh yes, we do. Sometimes, you just want something greasy, juicy, and hopelessly bad for you, and you want it fast."

I break into a fit of laughter, and I'm grateful for it. Hopefully, that will hide the shade of tomato red coloring my face.

"So, yeah," he continues with a grin. "This stuff is technically not good for you, but it's still *good*. Food is pleasure, after all. Besides, it doesn't make sense to prepare a big breakfast on a day like today. We're going to be eating all day long," he jokes. "Help yourself." He gestures to the rest of the baguette. "Or do you want something else? I can fix you—"

"No need," I reply with a smile. "This is great." Grabbing the knife, I spread some Nutella on my slice of bread. "So, are you from a family of chefs? What am I walking into?"

I bite the inside of my cheek, hating that I have to lie to him. But I also can't admit I know who his dad is. It might make him suspicious.

He scratches his beard. "Well, yes and no. My dad is a chef—was, technically—and he worked in kitchens his entire life. Most of the time in the kitchen I'm currently running, actually. I just took over a few months ago."

"Oh, okay," I say with a nod. "And your mom?"

"My mom didn't work outside the home. She was a hostess in my dad's first restaurant, but then they had me, and she quit. It's hard to raise children when both parents work in the hospitality industry."

"I can imagine, yeah."

"Then, there's my younger brother, Matt. He's a cop. His wife, Agathe, is a physiotherapist, and they have five-year-old twin girls, Juliette and Camille."

"Okay," I say, trying to absorb all of this info into my brain. "I can't promise I'll remember their names, but . . ."

He smiles, showcasing his dimple, and I avert my eyes again. "Don't worry. You're already being kind enough to do this for me. It doesn't matter if you remember their names."

I blush at the way his eyes size me up. Like they're devouring me with the same fervor as his teeth tearing into that slice of bread. "Of course. I mean, it's the least I can do after what you did for me. But, um, we really should put some ground rules in place for today, you know?"

"Rules?" he asks with a frown before drinking a sip of his coffee.

I shift in my seat, already regretting bringing it up. "Yes, that's what we're supposed to do, apparently, since we're—you know—fake dating?"

He arches an eyebrow. "Really? I didn't know there was a guide written about this."

"Trust me, neither did I." A light chuckle escapes me. "My sister, however, seems to know all about it."

His eyebrows shoot up. "You have a sister?"

"Ivy. She's a nurse. She called yesterday to make sure I was still alive, and that you didn't cut me into little pieces. I mentioned our arrangement for the day, and she said—"

"Wait. What? Cut you into pieces?" He shakes his head, his forehead wrinkled.

I wave a hand in dismissal. "Oh, don't worry. We're way past that now. The time we thought you were a serial killer is long gone," I tease.

He bursts into laughter. "Well, that's reassuring."

I roll my eyes with a smile. "I know. Anyway, she said we need to set some rules. It's mandatory, apparently."

He shoots me a smirk. "Well, if Ivy said it's mandatory, who am I to stand in her way?"

I suppress another chuckle. "Sorry. She watches too much TV. It's a problem."

"What kind of rules are we talking about?" he prods, standing up to clear the table.

"Mostly concerning PDA, I guess. Also, we have to get our story straight for when we tell your parents."

He places his mug in the sink, then turns to me. "Right."

After rinsing his mug, he scratches his chin. "Well, we met at the restaurant," he says. "We can pretty much stick to the true story to make it easier. Let's just say this was a month ago instead of two days. I did tell my mom our relationship was new, and she doesn't know anything about you except your nationality and name. You can just say that you're working here temporarily for the university? Maybe a six-month mission?"

"Whoa, okay. For someone who didn't think this through, you already have a pretty clear idea about what our story looks like," I joke.

He scrunches his nose. "Yeah, sorry. That's just how my brain works. Ideas leap from one to the next at lightspeed, and I can see the entire thing unraveling."

I place my chin in my hand. "Pretty cool."

"I guess. So, does that work? I think it's smart to go with the temporary mission here in Paris. That way, when they eventually learn we've broken up, they won't be surprised, and my mom won't try to chase you down."

"Oh gosh, yes. Great thinking." It's a good thing I'm not planning on moving here. I'd be afraid to run into his mom every time I went out. "Okay. We have that settled. What about PDA? How much is expected?"

He shifts his weight from one leg to the other, and I'm relieved to see this whole thing is a bit awkward for him too.

"I don't know. What are you comfortable with? We don't have to do anything you don't want to. It's only a family lunch, after all."

The way he just fretted about my feelings made my heart leap a few inches in my chest. Olivier really is a thoughtful guy. I don't know him well, but that facet of his personality is hopelessly endearing. And oddly refreshing. Neal was more a "let's do this" kind of guy. He was so pretentious that he didn't feel the need to seek my agreement on anything. Or care about what I thought. Just like his move to Australia.

I suck in a small breath. "Okay, yeah. Let's not go crazy. We can hold hands, I guess. You can have your arm around me, that kind of thing."

"Would you be okay with kissing me?" he asks, swallowing hard.

I open my mouth, but no sound comes out, probably because my brain is drawing blanks.

"Not with tongue or anything," he quickly amends, as if sensing my distress. "It's just that our relationship won't be believable if we don't kiss at least once. My mom already doesn't believe I'm really bringing someone, and she probably has that other girl on speed dial in case I show up alone. A kiss or two would guarantee she doesn't eye us with suspicion all day long."

"Right," I say, tucking a strand of hair behind my ear. "You can kiss me. Without tongue." I didn't even know that was possible in France. Yet another disappointing false cliché.

He wrings his hands in front of him. "Okay. Well, thank you."

"No, thank *you*," I say, my lips too tight to smile. "It's the least I can do to repay your generosity." I clear my throat. "So, we only have one rule, then? Stick to hand holding and kissing with no tongue?"

"I guess so. Do you have something to add?"

"Don't break rule number one?" I say, one eyebrow raised.

"Sounds good to me," he replies with the beginnings of a smirk.

I giggle softly, and as he walks toward the bathroom, my eyes zero in on his incredible *derrière*. Simmering heat takes over my body as I feel a tinge of regret. Why did I limit the PDA to hand holding?

Chapter 9

Olivier

Hazel and I are currently driving to my parents' house, and my body temperature still hasn't come back down. I'm starting to think I'm running a fever. Surely, if this was just the effect of our talk about sharing a kiss, the warmth would have passed at some point during the fifteen-minute cool shower I took this morning. To be fair, the water did calm my scorching-hot skin. But then, I strode back into the living area, and it all came surging back, as if my eyes still couldn't adjust to how stunning she looks today.

I cast her a quick glance now. She's wearing her brown hair down, but it's styled perfectly, framing her face that bears a touch of tasteful makeup. Her short black sweater dress flares above her knees, and her sheer tights make her legs shimmer. It's as if this dress has been tailor-made for her, highlighting every one of her gorgeous curves.

"So," she says. "What should I talk to them about? What are your family's interests? All you told me was their jobs."

I scratch my temple. "Right. Well, they don't exactly speak English very well, so I'm not sure how this whole thing is going to play out. My dad only knows basic words and kitchen vocabulary since he had a few foreign interns over the years. My mom has a better handle on it, I think. At least, she tells me she's watching most of her favorite shows in English with French subtitles, so that's something. Agathe is probably the one in my family with the most knowledge due to her studies, and Matt," I say with a chuckle. "I have no idea what words Matt knows in English, probably fewer than his daughters who watch *Dora the Explorer*."

"Oh, okay," she mutters, and I can sense she's getting nervous.

"Don't worry, though. It'll be fine. In a way, it's perfect, that way they won't bother you too much with awkward questions. And I'll be there to translate. I won't leave you alone."

I reach across the console to squeeze her leg like I would if she were my real girlfriend who I was trying to comfort. But then, I realize she's not, and she probably wouldn't want my hand on her thigh when there's no one around to convince, especially when she's wearing that short dress. I groan inwardly. What did I get myself into? Instead of squeezing her leg, my hand hangs mid-air for a few seconds before I rest it between us on the console. She looks at it for a beat but doesn't say anything, probably wondering what on earth I'm doing.

"Wait. Doesn't Dora teach Spanish, though? Because, believe it or not, my Spanish is even worse than my French," she says with a chuckle-snort.

My eyebrows scrunch together. "No, she teaches English. Doesn't she teach French in America?"

Hazel shakes her head. "Nope. Our kids learn Spanish from her."

A small laugh tumbles from my lips. "Huh! Who would have thought?"

"I know! Maybe she teaches French in Spanish-speaking countries?"

I rub my chin. "Mm. Highly doubt that. She probably teaches English everywhere outside of English-speaking countries."

"True. We like to have the language monopoly," she says with a cheeky smile that instantly puts my nerves at ease. Thank you, Dora, I guess. "So, is that how you learned English? Because if it is, the girl has a better method for teaching English than Spanish. Your English is virtually flawless."

I place both hands back on the wheel. "Oh, thank you," I reply, flashing a smile. "It's a nice compliment. I worked in kitchens all around the world these past seven years. Then, I decided to come back and settle down here. But it was a great experience."

"Wow. I can imagine. Where did you work?"

"Shanghai, Tokyo, Phuket, Dubai, Copenhagen, Milan, and Montreal."

Her eyes widen. "That's impressive! Not in the US, then?"

"No." I shake my head. "The opportunity never presented itself. But since English is the international language, and we already established that Dora teaches it everywhere, it was the language we always spoke in the kitchens. What about you? Have you traveled a lot for work, or is this your first time in Europe?"

"My first time," she says, looking out the window. "My boss actually wanted me to relocate here. That's part of why he sent me. And because I'm the only sad, single soul in my department, apparently. But I don't think it's a great fit."

My body tenses. *Way to go, Paris. Thanks for ruining it for her.* "Yeah, it's pretty bad timing. Paris is not the romantic city they portray in the movies by any means, but it's also not usually this bad."

"Yeah. Just bad timing," she repeats, her gaze settling on me for a few seconds before she turns to look outside again.

"At least it's a beautiful day," I say, pulling the sun visor down. "And the weather is supposed to stay sunny all through next week. Even if it's not Florida, I'd say it's not too bad for the last week of October."

"Yeah. That puts me in a good mood. Maybe this trip will finish on a better note. And those pretty fall colors will never get old."

And you might change your mind, I want to add, but I don't. She already thinks I'm unhinged.

I slow down as I turn onto my parents' street.

Hazel rubs her hands together. "Are we already here?"

"Yup. They don't live far. Here's their house," I say, pointing to the small residence with light-blue shutters and window boxes.

Once I park the car behind my brother's SUV, we get out and stroll toward the house. Hazel nervously wipes her palms on her dress, and I offer my hand to her. Hand holding is part of the agreement, after all, and I have a feeling it'll help with her anxiety.

As we approach the front door, I suddenly don't feel so confident about my brilliant plan. Sure, it'll get my mom off my back for the moment and avoid me having to go on a date with Justine Gardinet, but I feel bad for Hazel. I practically forced her into this. She was too polite to say no after I offered her a room. I had no ill intent when I asked, of course, but that's just how it worked out.

"I'm sorry," I say, turning to her. "I realize how crazy this entire thing is."

Her smile warms my heart. "It's fine. I understand why we're doing this. Plus, the house looks gorgeous!"

I glance back toward my parents' home. Mom always goes overboard when it comes to decorations. Large wooden planters filled with orange flowers and big pumpkins frame the pathway to the front door, and a friendly scarecrow holding a "welcome" sign is staked in a haystack near the mailbox. Topping it off is an autumn wreath adorning the front door. Oh, I forgot to mention the burgundy-leaf garland draping the bushes. And this is relatively low-key. You should see it at Christmastime.

"Yeah. I hope you're starving, because Mom always goes all out for her birthday," I say, guiding Hazel toward the front door.

"Oh, your mom is the one cooking?" She tips her head to the side. "I thought it'd be your dad."

"Right," I chuckle. "I forget that the dynamic is kind of weird. My dad never cooks at home. But don't worry, my mom's cuisine is full of flavor and generosity."

"Oh, I'm not worried one bit. Let's do this, *boyfriend*." She squeezes my hand. "Though you could have offered to cook for your mom's birthday!" she scolds.

I swallow hard, trying to ignore the warm tingling that's traveling up my arm. "Oh, trust me. I wanted to. But she always refuses. No one is allowed to cook in her kitchen or for her guests. Probably her way of proving to us that you don't have to be a chef to be an excellent cook."

"I love her already," Hazel chirps, tugging my hand as we reach the front door.

Another current of tingling energy courses through my arm. I really hope she does. I hope she clicks with all of them, and that in return, they see how amazing Hazel is.

I kick a pebble on the stoop, and it bounces against the door. It might as well have landed on my forehead because I'm suddenly hit in the face by reality. None of this is genuine, so it doesn't matter if they hate each other's guts. Something must be wrong with me. Why do I even care? She's practically a stranger, and she's leaving in a few days. I shouldn't give a hoot if they get along or not. Actually, you know what? I don't. At least, that's what I repeat to myself as my knuckles rap on the door.

Hazel

My heart thrums harder and harder in its cage as Olivier knocks on the door. *It'll be fine,* I tell myself. People who decorate their house for fall with wreaths and garlands can't be monsters, right?

The door flies open, and a plump woman with a beaming smile opens the door. She exudes mixed vibes of Molly Weasley from *Harry Potter* and Mrs. Patmore from *Downton Abbey.*

"*Enfin, vous voilà!*" she greets, opening her arms wide to take her son into a hug. When they break the embrace, she places a kiss on each of his cheeks.

"*Bon anniversaire, Maman,*" he says. "*Je te présente, Hazel, ma petite amie. Hazel ne parle pas bien français.*" He turns to me. "Hazel, this is Joelle, my mom."

I stick my hand out. "Happy—"

Joelle surprises me by pulling me into a tight hug, just like she did her son. And I get the kisses too. Yup, definitely your typical overbearing mother. Well, the kisses are honestly a bit much, but I go along with it.

"Hello, Hazel. Beautiful name. *Enchantée*."

Her accent is thick. Definitely the typical French accent I encountered during my trip, but with a roundness to it.

"*Enchantée*," I echo back with a dip of my head. "And Happy Birthday."

She claps her hands together, her gaze raking my body. "Thank you. Please, come inside."

We follow her into the house, and it's as cute on the inside as it was on the outside. The whole neighborhood has this quaint village atmosphere, between the colorful trees, the cobblestone streets, and the cute houses with pumpkin-lined windowsills.

We hang our coats in the hallway before stepping into a large living room and dining area where a hardwood table has been set up for lunch. The fall theme is still going strong in here, and the festive atmosphere instantly makes me feel at home. My mom was always big on decorating too, but Christmas was her favorite holiday. Taking in the spread, I spot a few carved pumpkin decorations, various potpourris on the consoles, and a table runner with a patchwork of leaves. In the middle of the dining table stands a giant flower arrangement made of deep burgundy and burnt-orange dahlias, sprigs of goldenrod, and clusters of miniature pumpkins.

Behind the table, a floor-to-ceiling window opens to an outdoor deck, and I hear the shouts and giggles of children playing from afar.

"Philippe," Joelle yells, and a grunt carries from the upper level.

"J'arrive," a gruff voice responds.

"My 'usband is coming," Joelle says with a warm smile.

"*Où sont Agathe et Matt*?" Olivier asks, looking around. "My brother," he explains to me. I don't get it at first, but then his mom speaks a few words, pointing to the backyard, and I understand he's looking for his brother.

"Let's go say hi," he says.

I let him guide me outside, my hand still firmly wrapped in his. A wave of electricity zipped through me when we first touched, but now that I've gotten used to it, his firm grip is a welcome comfort.

"*Ah, Olive est là,*" a tall, lanky guy calls out, walking toward us. "*Salut, mec,*" he says to his brother, and they greet each other with a brotherly handshake. Olivier's brother looks like a younger version of him.

"*Voici Hazel,*" Olivier says, taking a step back to stand next to me. "Hazel, this is my brother, Matthieu, but you can call him Matt."

"*Bonjour,*" I say with a timid smile.

"'Ello," he says before venturing a step toward me, placing two kisses on my cheeks. I remain rigid, having trouble grasping the need for this family to assault strangers with their mouths. Don't they usually reserve this greeting for the people they're close with? Then, the image of Olivier assaulting me with his own mouth flashes through my brain. Suddenly, it doesn't feel like an invasion of privacy anymore. I shake the intrusive thoughts away.

"*Ah, salut,*" a blonde woman wearing a dark-green jumpsuit says, rounding the corner from the side of the house with a bunch of toys in her hands. "*On est arrivé il y a vingt minutes et elles ont déjà fait le bazar,*" she says with an exasperated voice, shaking her head.

Olivier turns to me. "She said they've been here twenty minutes, and the girls have already made a mess."

"Ah." Yeah, that makes sense.

Olivier kisses her on both cheeks and—yup—it doesn't feel *that* weird after all. "*Salut, Agathe. C'est Hazel, ma petite amie.*"

"Oh!" she says, stepping around Olivier to greet me. And yes, she kisses me too. "*Salut, comment ça va?*"

"*Elle ne parle pas français,*" Matt says to his wife. "*Elle est américaine.*"

"Sorry," Agathe says. "Nice to meet you. Welcome to France."

"Thank you," I say, feeling a bit more at ease now that someone else speaks the same language as me.

"*Les filles,*" Matt says, turning around to catch sight of the two girls scrambling across the yard with their dolls clutched tightly. They are beyond cute with their matching orange dresses and pigtails. "*Oncle Olive est arrivé.*"

They stop what they're doing, their heads snapping to where we stand. They come running straight into their uncle's arms, their dark-blonde pigtails bouncing.

I don't understand a word their little voices are saying, partly because weird things are happening to my body as I watch the way Olivier spins them in the air and talks to them.

"*Les filles,*" Olivier says, squatting down to their level. "*Dites bonjour à Hazel.*"

Olivier stands up, and his sparkling eyes meet mine. "Hazel, my nieces, Camille and Juliette."

"*Bonjour*," I say with a timid wave. French children are even more intimidating than French adults. They can't understand yet why I'm this weird person who doesn't speak their language.

"*Hazel est américaine*," he says. "Do you know any words in English?"

He casts a quick glance at Agathe, who nods.

"Hello?" Juliette peeps, cocking her head to the side.

"*Très bien*," Olivier says, high-fiving her.

"*Je le savais aussi*," the other girl says, clearly feeling rejected.

"*C'est bien*," Olivier says, high-fiving her the same way. "She said she knew that as well."

I nod. I still suck at speaking, but I'm getting better at understanding, at least.

"And 'thank you'," Camille adds.

"There you go," Olivier says, standing up. "I told you my nieces knew more words than my brother."

Agathe and I chuckle, and Matt peers at his brother, eyes squinting. "*Tu parles de moi, n'est-ce pas?*"

"*Pas du tout*. I'm not talking about you at all," he says, winking at me. "Ah, Dad." His eyes lift to something above my head. I turn around to see a tall man with a square jaw and an imposing frame. He looks like a mix between Olivier and Matthieu, but he doesn't have that gleam of mischief in his eyes.

Olivier introduces us, and I try to smile. I take back what I said about the girls being the most intimidating of the bunch. Philippe definitely beats his granddaughters in that department. The way he looks at me—while not mean or anything—exudes confidence, seriousness, and respect.

They all start chatting in French. I try to follow, but they're talking way too fast, and I quickly lose the thread.

When the girls go scurrying to the side of the house, Agathe and Matt follow them. I take the small respite to turn to Olivier. "Can I ask you something?"

He nods. "Of course."

"What's with all the kissing?" My cheeks warm as the question leaves my lips.

"Oh." He chuckles, revealing his sexy dimple. "I forgot how French that is. It's called *faire la bise*. That's just how we greet each other in a casual setting. When we're in a professional environment, we shake hands like everyone else. Sorry, I should have told them to—"

"No, no." I place a hand on his shoulder. "It's perfectly fine. I'm the one who needs to adapt, that's all. It took me by surprise, I guess. I thought it was only for close friends and family."

He scratches the back of his head. "My bad. I should have warned you. And no, we basically greet everyone like that."

"Oh, wow. Okay."

"Good thing that here in Paris, it's only two kisses," he says with a grin. "In some regions, they do three or four."

That's a lot of kisses, though if it were with Olivier, the number wouldn't seem that high after all.

The door to the back porch opens, and Joelle's face appears through it. *"C'est prêt,"* she says. *"A table."*

The girls come running from the corner of the house, screaming their lungs out.

Olivier turns to me. "She said—"

"Oh, I know what that one means. We're eating now."

A large grin splashes across his face as he motions me into the house ahead of him.

Chapter 10

Hazel

The elaborate spread Joelle prepared is sumptuous, and she definitely cooks at a professional level. *Boeuf bourguignon* with a truffle, butternut, and potato purée. She might not be the chef of the household, but she can hold her own in the kitchen. I spend most of the meal gushing *"très bien"* or *"délicieux,"* because those are the only ways I know how to give compliments in French. Not very elaborate, but it seems to do the trick, because Joelle beams every time a word leaves my mouth.

The three men are carrying an animated conversation, and I don't understand a word of it. Distress must be written all over my face, because Agathe, who's sitting across from me, says, "Don't worry. They're just talking about football."

"Oh, right," I say with an amused smile.

"Well, soccer for you, I guess," she says. "But anyway, it's all the same. Just men talking sports."

"Yeah, that's a global phenomenon," I joke.

"*Exactement*. You've been in Paris for a long time, yes?" she asks as Joelle brings the dessert to the table, asking for each of our plates to serve us.

"A few months," I say, not wanting to get too specific. "I'm here on a six-month mission for work."

"Oh, what do you do?"

"I'm a historian," I say, swallowing the dry lump in my throat. It'll never feel normal to say that. I really need to do some research. I conducted a few searches online, but I didn't really know where to start. I mean, what's my specialty? What period am I studying? I need more info. I probably should have chosen a job I actually had a clue about. My lack of common sense baffles me sometimes.

"Oh, cool. Then Paris must be a great city for you. What are you working on right now?"

"Oh," I mumble, my cheeks burning. Thankfully, Joelle just placed a plate in front of me before taking her seat again at the end of the table. I pivot to face her. *"Merci, Joelle."*

"*De rien. Goûte,*" she says, probing me to give it a taste. She doesn't need to tell me twice. Joelle made a delicate chocolate profiterole, and it's divine.

"Mm, *très délicieux,*" I say.

The beaming smile returns to her face. "Thank you. You like French cuisine?" she asks, nodding rapidly as her eyes glow with eagerness.

"Oh, yes," I reply, relieved that the conversation shifted. "*Oh oui, très beaucoup.* French cuisine is the best."

With a big smile, she looks at Olivier who's on my left, still talking to his brother and father. *"Alors,* you are coming to the autumn festival next week?" she asks. That gets Olivier's attention.

"*Oh, non, Maman. Hazel travaille. Elle ne peut pas venir.*"

"You must work?" She observes me with a deep frown. "But it's the weekend. Weekend is for fun, not work. You must come."

I wipe my mouth with my napkin, then turn to Olivier. "What's the autumn festival?"

"It's an event hosted by the girls' school to finance their school trip. The festival is next week, but you don't have to come."

"Yes, come," Joelle encourages with a large grin, clearly not missing a beat of our conversation.

"You really should check it out," Agathe adds with a nod. "It's always a great time. There are vendors selling homemade products and—of course—plenty of food," she says, glancing at Olivier.

"You're cooking?" I tilt my head to look at him.

"Yes. I actually have the week off work so I can prepare for it. It's a big event, but you really don't—"

"Olivier," Joelle cuts in. "She is your lover. She—"

"I'd love to come," I blurt. Olivier's mouth falls open.

I don't know if it's because I'm dying to taste more of his cooking, or because I can't resist a fall festival surrounded by actual fall colors—not exactly the same picture in Florida—or if the word "lover" spilling from Joelle's mouth kickstarted it all. But there, I said it.

"Are you sure?" Olivier murmurs, his eyes trying to decipher what's going on in my brain and searching for hidden meaning behind my eyes.

"Positive," I say with a nod. "It sounds like fun."

He relaxes into his chair. "Okay, then."

"And *of course* you are coming to Joelle's Halloween party on Friday night," Agathe adds.

I blink back. "Oh . . ."

"Certainly, they are coming," Joelle confirms, her eyes flitting between her son and me. "Olivier never misses my party."

He opens his mouth, probably to decline, but I cut him off. *"Oui*, we are coming." What's one more event at this point? Plus, Joelle is so nice, it's impossible to turn her down. You don't refuse anything to Molly Weasley. Or Mrs. Patmore.

"Super," Joelle gushes, clapping her hands together before getting up to clear the table.

Olivier leans into me. "You don't have to say yes to everything my mother asks, you know," he whispers in my ear, sending chills through my body.

"I know," I whisper back. "But you can't miss your mom's big event either. And anyway, it's fine. Everyone likes a party. I don't mind."

"Okay," he says with a dip of his head before getting up to help his mom.

Once we're done clearing the table, we all step back outside to enjoy some fresh air. The girls are playing with their hula hoops, and Phillipe is raking leaves while Agathe, Joelle, and I sit around a rattan table, chatting about our favorite TV shows. Thankfully, Agathe is playing translator.

As Agathe and Joelle share a few words in French, my phone pings, telling me I've got an Instagram notification, so I check it out. It's a picture of Neal and his new girlfriend kissing in front of their newly opened surf shop in Australia. I turn off notifications for his account and shut my screen off, not even bothering to read the caption.

"*Excusez moi*," I mumble to Joelle and Agathe before quickly retreating to the restroom. My stomach twists, the picture still fresh in my mind. We broke up months ago, but seeing him so happy, living his dream, reminds me how far apart our lives are. *My time will come,* I remind myself, repeating it like a mantra. Having gotten lost looking for the restroom, I end up in a corridor with several doors on each side. One is slightly ajar, and deep voices carry into the hallway. It's Olivier and his brother. I'm about to turn around, because I'm pretty sure this isn't the right way, when I hear Matt say my name followed by the word "canon."

Olivier sighs. "*Oh, oui. Elle est vraiment canon.*" They both chuckle at that, and I don't hear the rest of the sentence.

Fearing they might step out of the room, I retrace my steps to where I came from, and Camille—I think—emerges from one of the doorways, her dress stuck in her underwear. She looks at me for a second, like she's done something wrong.

"Do you need some help?" I ask, but the little girl just runs away.

Well, at least now I know where the bathroom is.

After finishing my business, I open the browser on my phone to look up the word "canon" because I can't stop thinking about it. I lean against the door next to the restroom as I type on my phone.

First, a bunch of printers, cameras, and related equipment come up. Right, it's a Japanese electronics company.

Next, I try *"canon c'est quoi,"* and I mostly come across pictures of actual cannons. That's what came to mind at first, but this doesn't make any sense. Why would he call me a cannon?

Olivier

"Hey," I say when I spot Hazel near the restroom as I'm going back outside, Matt close on my heels. "What are you doing here?"

"Nothing," she rushes, hastily turning off her phone's screen. "How are you?"

I frown, not sure what all that fluster was about. "Good."

She looks to the right, and I notice my mom pretending to dust the shelf while sneaking glances at us.

I bring my eyes back to Hazel.

"Your mom is looking," she whispers, her cheeks turning pink.

"She is."

"You should kiss me." When the words leave her mouth, I almost choke on my saliva. I place a hand on the wall to steady myself, which also brings me closer to her. "Are you sure?"

Her eyes remain locked on mine, and she nods. "It'll be weird if you don't. She's expecting it."

"Right."

I stare at Hazel a beat longer, trying to gather the courage. But no matter how long I wait, I'm pretty sure I'll never be ready for what's about to happen. Because her lips look more delicious than any meal I've ever tasted.

Swallowing hard, I lean toward her, and she tilts her head back. Her eyes flutter closed, but I can't follow suit. I need to see every part of this. I capture her chin in my hand and place a soft kiss on her lips. I let my mouth linger for a few seconds, intending to break apart after a moment, but I can't do it. Instead, I step closer and wrap my arms around her waist, deepening the kiss. She responds by lacing her hands behind my neck. Warmth spreads through my body, and I force myself to take a step back before I accidentally take this even further. We did say no tongue, after all, and the whole thing is just pretend. She opens her eyes, and her gaze meets mine. For a second, I think I detect a fiery flicker mirroring the flame raging inside of me, but then, she shoots a glance to the right to see if my mom is still there. She turns back to me with a knowing look and a thin smile.

I break away, forcing a grin. Taking her hand in mine, I guide her back outside, hoping my racing heart will settle down.

The rest of the afternoon goes pretty well. It almost feels like Hazel has been here for years. Right now, she's laughing with Agathe and my mom, which doesn't help with my heart rate. I've been looking for this my entire life. An honest woman who I share interests with, who I can laugh with. A woman who would get along well with my parents and understands the demands of my work. But I remind myself that Hazel is not that person. While we do have a lot in common, and she's always up for a good laugh, she's not my real girlfriend. This is just a favor. After one week, two if I'm lucky, she'll go back to her life, and I'll remain stuck in mine.

The sun is dipping low, and it's getting chilly outside. Matt and Agathe call it a day, with Hazel and me following close behind. Right now, I'm waiting for her near the entryway as she uses the restroom.

"I like Hazel," my mom declares in English, clearly improving by the second. "She is *magnifique, superbe. Une vraie femme*, with curves and substance. *Pas comme les brindilles avec qui tu étais avant.*"

I nod, agreeing completely. Hazel is nothing like any other woman I've ever met, let alone dated. Now that I think of it, I have mostly gone out with rather thin women. Not thin like a rake, like mom is suggesting, but still. Hazel's body is perfection. Her curves are exquisite, a gorgeous reflection of the love that she and I share of food. She looks healthy and full. *"A woman of substance,"* like my mom said, and she's exactly right.

Chapter 11

Hazel

Olivier and I are lounging on the couch, the TV on in the background. He's reading a magazine, and I'm scrolling on my phone. You'd think hanging out like this would be painfully awkward, especially since we shared a kiss earlier. A kiss I didn't want to break. A kiss I was dying to deepen just to see where it would lead. But surprisingly, I'm perfectly at ease. It's like I've known him all my life.

That kiss, though. Best twelve seconds of my life—not that I counted or anything. I almost moaned when he broke away. But that was for the best. This whole thing is strictly platonic.

"Can I ask you something?" I venture, unable to get what he said to his brother out of my head.

"Sure," he says, turning to look at me.

"What does *canon* mean?"

He frowns. "What?"

"*Canon*. You said I was *canon* to your brother," I mention, my face warming. "I overheard you while I was looking for the restroom."

He scratches his beard. "Oh."

I drill him with an expectant look, and he lowers his eyes back to his magazine. I knew it. It's something bad.

"Tell me."

"It means you're hot." He swallows hard, making his Adam's apple bob.

"Oh," I say, my mouth hanging open. I must be red as a cherry tomato by now, and Olivier is clearly as uncomfortable as I am, refusing to look me in the eye. No, no, no. This is not what platonic should look like.

"Well, thank you, I guess," I pipe up again, hoping to defuse the tension.

He finally locks eyes with me, and a smile spreads across his face. "*De rien.*"

"That's 'you're welcome,' right?"

He nods. "You're getting better."

I choke out a laugh. "Still have a long way to go before I'm fluent. Hopefully, I'll be better by the fall festival, or I'm going to be the town's laughingstock."

A tiny wrinkle appears on his forehead. "You were serious about going, then?"

"Why? Do you not want me to come? I guess I kind of invited myself without consulting you, huh? Sorry."

"*Non*. Of course I want you to come," he says quickly. "I'm just saying you don't *have* to."

"I want to. I love a good fall festival, especially when there's French food involved." I wink. "I'd be crazy to turn it down."

"Okay." He settles back into the couch. "I figured you just said yes to make my mom happy."

"I did, but also to make my stomach happy," I say, patting my belly.

"Well, good, then. I think you'll like the festival. It's a fun event, and the food is always the highlight of the day—though of course, I'm extremely biased." He throws me a side glance that makes me giggle.

"What are you going to make? Can I help?"

"I don't know yet," he says, closing his magazine. "It's only my third time catering it, and I try to do something different every year. I haven't really had time to think about it yet because of work. But that's why I took the week off. Tomorrow, I'll go to the market and see what I can do. And of course you can help, if you'd like, but don't you have to work?"

My stomach plunges to my socks. "Oh, no. Just a few things to write, but nothing huge. I was also really hoping to visit some more restaurants while I'm stuck here, but they're all booked up."

"Which ones did you want to try?"

"*La Rue*, *Opulence*, or *Gabriel Morin*, but they all turned me down."

"I'll get you a table," he says, as if it's the easiest thing in the world. "Don't worry about it."

My mouth falls open. "Really?"

He chuckles. "Of course. I know the owners very well. In fact, Gabriel Morin is one of my best friends. We were in school together. I'll text all three and ask for a table. Which day were you thinking of going?"

Could this man be more attractive? He's now getting me into the restaurants of my choice with nothing more than a couple of texts?

"When are you free?" I ask with a smile. "If you want to come, that is. Since you're not working."

He pauses for a second. Just when I think I'm about to receive a world-class rejection, he says, "Of course I want to come. I'm a chef. I never say no to food." He gives me a wink.

"Great," I say with a grin, a flood of relief washing over me. Not because he didn't say no, but because Jeff will be pleased that I can keep doing my job this week. Or at least, that's what I'm repeating to myself as I try to get to sleep. Forget counting sheep. This is the new way to lull myself into oblivion.

Olivier

The farmer's market is my favorite place on earth. No matter what country I'm in, I always end up smack in the middle of one. Of course, my prejudiced heart will always prefer the French markets. But can you really blame me?

I love meandering through the alleys, touching the fresh produce and artisanal food creations with all their perfect imperfections, breathing in their aromas and talking with the people who bring them to life. Everything about it is inspiring, like taking a stroll through paradise. This time, I even take in the beautiful fall colors. How did I not notice them before? With all the trees surrounding the square, the autumn leaves are absolutely gorgeous.

Hazel's eager eyes widen further with each step we take and each stall we visit.

"You know everyone here," she says, finishing off a piece of cheese Pierre gave her. "Do you come often?"

"Most days," I say with a smile. It's become one of my daily routines, a way to get inspired.

"Whoa, you're lucky. What a fantastic way to start your day."

"It is. How can someone not be inspired by all of this fresh produce? The colors, the smells, the passion of the people who grow and select them. This is what cooking is all about, you know?"

"Believe me, I'm with you." She takes a long breath of the cool morning air. "So, do we have everything we need? All this sampling has made me hungry," she jokes.

"I think so," I say, checking my tote bag one more time. "Oh, wait. Apples. We need apples."

She quirks an eyebrow. "We've already got cheese, mushrooms, and smoked ham. And now *apples*?"

"Trust me," I say with a secretive smirk.

We stop at Marie's stall for the apples before strolling back home. Living on the outskirts of the city is just like living in a village, but only half an hour from the capital. The best of both worlds.

Back home, we set up everything in the kitchen, and I grab us two aprons. I put on my fall one—with pumpkins, leaves, and mushrooms, and give her the Christmas one, which features candy canes, Christmas trees, and snowflakes.

"Do you only have seasonal aprons?" she asks as she ties the back.

"*Bien sûr*. That's how you get in the right mood."

Pulling my knives out, I begin sharpening them like I always do before I start any serious cooking session. She just stares at me, wearing an intense look on her face.

"Sorry for the noise," I say. "But you can't make great cuisine with bad equipment."

"No, it's fine," she says, a slight blush coloring her cheeks. "Where do you want me? Wait, what are we even making?"

"We're making portobello mushrooms stuffed with *fourme d'ambert*—the blue cheese we picked up—plus smoked ham, pine nuts, and apples."

"Sounds delish." She licks her lips, and I wish she hadn't. This platonic thing is excruciating enough as it is.

I tear my eyes away. "Right, okay. You can begin by washing the mushrooms and the apples. I'll start on the cheese."

Cooking with Hazel feels surprisingly natural, and she's a great sous chef. She doesn't stand in my way and always lends a helping hand. She has great instincts too. When I told her to watch the apples as they were cooking, she knew just when to take it off the fire.

Once we finish, I take the dish out of the oven and probe the mushroom with my finger. "Yep. It's done."

She offers me a warm smile, and I can tell she's as eager as I am to taste it.

I serve us two plates, and she gets us a pitcher of water from the fridge. We're about to have our first bite when I say, "Stop."

"Why?" she whines, her hands falling loudly on the table with a slap.

"I forgot the final touch. Hold on."

Getting up, I grab the pine nuts and crush them meticulously.

"You're killing me," she groans with a light chuckle.

"Just wait." Hustling back to the kitchen bar, I sprinkle a few pine nuts over her dish, then mine. "Okay, now we can eat."

I cut my mushroom in two halves and gaze appreciatively at the way the cheese melts on my plate. Then, I try it. As always when I eat something, I analyze every element of the dish. The mushroom bursts with savory flavor, and the texture is perfect, firm but a little squishy. The strong personality of the cheese takes over, but it's toned down by the sweet and sour taste of the apple. The smoked ham brings a meaty taste and a touch of crispiness, and the pine nuts crunch under the teeth, finishing the game of textures on the palate.

"Mmm," Hazel moans, her eyes still closed when I open mine. "This is amazing. And it didn't even take that long to make. I'll *have* to steal this recipe."

"Thanks," I say with an exaggerated sigh. "Finally, something I make that you like. Disaster averted."

She gives me a pointed look as she takes another bite of stuffed mushroom. "Come on, we've talked about this. Plus, I liked breakfast the other day, remember?"

"Yeah," I say, raising my eyes to meet hers. "But I'm a chef, and breakfast isn't my specialty. This is."

"Darn right it is."

I don't say anything. Instead, I just smile. It's a real smile too, one that's impossible to break. A smile that stretches from ear to ear and showcases all your teeth. Because as much as seeing other people enjoying my dishes is a treat, seeing Hazel revel in my cooking is without a doubt the best sensation in the world.

Chapter 12

Hazel

Since I keep forgetting to ask Olivier if I can use his washing machine, I get dressed in my last clean outfit—a black tube skirt with a red blouse—and slip into my stilettos. I apply some red lipstick and check myself in the mirror, just like I would if I were going on a date.

But *you are not going on a date, Hazel. It's just a— A . . . Well, whatever this is, it's not a date. That's all I know.*

Taking a deep breath, I step out of "my" bedroom. Olivier is leaning against the kitchen bar, scrolling on his phone. He glances toward me.

"Wow," he says. "You look *magnifique*."

"Oh, this?" I say, looking down and pretending I dress like this every night. Which I don't. "It's nothing."

"Oh, it's something," he says, his eyes raking my body.

"No, it's really not," I say, my cheeks suddenly burning. The last thing I need is for him to think *I think* this is a date. "But we are going to a triple Michelin-starred restaurant, so I have to dress up a little bit."

He nods. "Right. Should we go, then?"

"Yes. Oh, one more thing. Could I use your washing machine tomorrow? I'm running out of clean clothes."

"Of course you can. Anything you need," he says, opening the front door to let me through.

"Thanks," I say, blushing a few shades deeper as he steps in front of me to close the door behind us. Why am I so shy about asking to wash my clothes at his place? I've been eating his home cooking and sleeping next door to him. There's something seriously wrong with me.

"By the way, are you using my body wash?" he asks, cocking his head to the side.

My cheeks are now a pair of hot frying pans. "Maybe." He chuckles and shakes his head.

"It's because I'm out of shower gel," I lie. In truth, I haven't touched mine since I got here. His is just too addictive. "Sorry."

"No, it's fine. Do you want me to take you to the store so you can buy some? Or I can show you the way if you want to go alone."

"Oh no, I'm fine. I actually like yours. It smells nice. If you don't mind me using it, of course," I add, realizing I've already taken enough advantage of his generosity.

"No. Feel free to use it," he says, wringing his hands. "I don't mind at all. It smells nice on you. Anyway, we should really get going." He breathes a chuckle, but it sounds more like a nervous laugh.

I swallow hard as I follow him to the car. Could this be any more awkward?

Olivier is pulling the car into a parking spot when my phone rings. Jeff again. This is his fourth time calling today, and even if he is a cool boss, I'm going to be out of a job soon if I don't answer him.

"Hey, Jeff," I say when I pick up the phone. Then, I mouth "my boss" to Olivier, who nods in understanding before turning the ignition off.

"Hazel! How are you doing? Did you manage to score reservations?" Jeff asks, his usual cheery tone bursting through the phone.

"I'm good. Yes, I did," I say, stealing a glance at Olivier.

"Fantastic. Which ones?"

I get out of the car as he's talking, and I slam the door a bit harshly behind me. Turning around, I notice Olivier has already gotten out as well. There goes my plan of blurting the name of the restaurant incognito.

"What did you say?" I frown, pressing my hand against my ear. "I can't hear you well. Service is terrible."

Great excuse, Hazel. You're in the middle of Paris.

"I said, which restaurants?"

"Oh, um. I'm not sure how to pronounce the names, but I'll send you a text right away, okay?" My heart is rattling in my chest, and my body feels hot under my blouse. I'm not the best liar. Ironic, since I've been doing just that nonstop for a few days now.

"Yeah, okay," Jeff says, his voice lilting in confusion. "I'll be looking forward to your reviews. You did a great job with the ones from last week. They should be live on the website in no time."

My eyes widen, and I'm suddenly sweating. "Oh, already? I'm sure there are still a lot of edits to work on. Paris is messing with my brain. Actually, if you don't mind, I was thinking I could take a look at them again."

I know I shouldn't attempt to stop my reviews from being posted just because I'm now friends with the chef. It's completely unethical. I ate at Olivier's restaurant on the company payroll and reviewed his cuisine with an objective eye. Even if that meal wasn't representative of his talents, that's the meal I had to judge. I hate that I just asked Jeff for this favor, but I couldn't help myself. It's a lot harder to follow my code of ethics when Olivier is standing a few feet away from me, staring back at me with his usual kind eyes. He's a decent man. A good man. An excellent chef who deserves recognition. And I don't want to hurt him.

"What are you talking about?" Jeff asks, his confusion clearly mounting. "What could you possibly change? You did great, as always. Very detailed and fair. Once it's edited, it'll be posted online. I'll let you know."

"Okay," I peep, glancing at Olivier. He frowns, and I force myself to plaster on a big smile. Then, I jerk my head, indicating we can start walking. The fact that he's staring at me doesn't help.

"All right. Send me the next ones as soon as you can," my boss chirps.

I swallow to wet my dry throat. "Sure. Bye, Jeff."

Once I end the call, I stay silent, trying to digest the conversation and the dose of reality that just slapped me in the face. "Are you okay?" Olivier asks, shooting me a concerned glance.

I shake my thoughts into focus and force another grin. "Yes, sorry. It was my supervisor. You know how bosses are."

His frown dissolves into an empathetic smile. "I do. I'm sorry if I've kept you from your work, and if I made you late for anything. It wasn't my intention."

"Don't be," I say, my smile genuine this time. "I loved cooking with you, and don't worry, you haven't made me late for anything."

It just keeps getting harder and harder to hide who I really am from this man.

When we arrive at the restaurant, I fully intend to put my work face on. But the guilt is eating me alive. Jeff's phone call reminded me that I'm only here for one reason—work. At the same time, my presence here tonight is solely thanks to my new friend, Olivier. How can I ignore him and focus on my job in this situation? It's impossible. Drawing a deep breath, I try to focus, but when Olivier has his hand on the small of your back, guiding you to your table, focusing is impossible. Try it, I dare you.

The restaurant is beautiful, all dressed in white and beige with wood accents to warm up the space. We're seated in the far corner of the room, which opens to a view of the sparkling Eiffel Tower. Ivy would approve.

We order the tasting menu, and Olivier chooses, with the help of the sommelier, a nice bottle of wine to pair with our dinner.

His phone buzzes with a notification, and he grabs it from his pocket. "Sorry. I'll put it on silent. Oh, wait, it's

Mom." A smile lights up his face as he texts her back. "She loved you. Just like I knew she would, so thank you again." Tucking his phone away, he raises his glass to me.

"My pleasure," I say as I clink my glass with his. "I had a great time."

"Hopefully, her faith in me will be restored, and that will last well after our 'breakup,'" he says. "Then, I'll be off the hook for a while."

I laugh even as my stomach sinks. "You *really* don't want a girlfriend, do you?"

He pauses, looking thoughtful. Just as he's about to speak, the waiter brings us our first dish. Braised scallops with caviar and a creamy parsnip sauce. We both take a bite and appreciate the flavors. It's truly fantastic. The marriage of the earthy and saline flavors is a surprising hit, and the texture of the *velouté* is addictive.

"Do you like it?" he asks.

"I do. The *velouté* is comforting, and the caviar and scallops add a touch of pep."

"I couldn't have said it better myself. Try the wine with it," he says, taking a sip. "To answer your question, I have nothing against dating. It's just not the right time for me. I only got back a year ago, and I'm working in a new place, trying to find my footing. In fact, this is the first time I've had a vacation in—well—a year. So this is definitely not representative of my regular routine," he jokes. "I do go to the farmer's market and cook, but after that, I have little time to relax since I have to drive into the city and start cooking again for the entire night. During my days off, I work on dishes at home, or I see my family, but my life is mostly work."

"I see what you mean. I'm in the same boat, and it's a rocky one. I don't know what my boss will say when I admit I don't want the job here," I say with a sigh. "All his hopes are resting on me. I wanted the promotion, but I don't know. It just doesn't feel right."

He eats the last bites of his dish. "Is that why you're not dating?"

"Not really. My job allows me personal time, and I have actually dated since my last long-term relationship ended—when my ex chose a skinny blonde and a surfboard over me—but it was one failure after the next. It was like the more I pushed for it, the worse it got. So, I just stopped trying altogether and embraced the single life," I say with an awkward chuckle.

"I'll drink to that," Olivier says, raising his glass again before bringing it to his lips. "To being single."

Olivier

As our dinner progresses, I'm more and more impressed by Hazel's vast knowledge of food. She knows most of the spices and plants we talk about, even the more uncommon and complex ones, like woodruff and *cistre*—AKA, the Alps' fennel.

"How do you know so much about cooking and flavors?" I finally ask when the server comes to take our last dish away. "I've never met anyone who's not in the industry with that much knowledge."

Her face turns pink, and it might just be my new favorite color. "Oh, um, I guess it just became a passion over the years. I just love eating so much."

"Still," I say, nodding appreciatively. "It's wonderful, all the things you know. And you're so good at identifying flavors. You have a good palate."

Her blush deepens, her long lashes covering her eyes as she looks down. I'm starting to wonder why she doesn't appreciate the compliment when she raises her eyes with a coy smile. "What, you mean for an American?"

A lighthearted laugh escapes me. "Not at all. I don't even know many French people who know what *cistre* is, for example."

And that knack for ingredients only increases her attractiveness—something I didn't think possible. But I must be delusional. Hazel doesn't want to date anyone, and *I* don't want to date anyone, so let's not go there. Plus, as soon as the strike ends, she'll be out of here, and the last thing I need right now is a broken heart. I'm having enough creativity problems at work as it is.

"Well, thank you," she finally says as the waiter brings the end-of-meal mini pastries. "It's actually my mom who got me into cooking. She *looooved* food." She pauses, her finger tracing the rim of her glass as a smile tugs at her lips. "She introduced us to high gastronomy at a very young age. Every time there was a special occasion, we'd go out to dinner to celebrate. We also cooked a lot together, and she was very inventive and creative in her cuisine. We'd scour the market for new ingredients and try new recipes all the time. Ivy and I had a blast, but I was the one who was really passionate about it. I would buy recipe books with my allowance and look online for the best spots to eat."

As she speaks, warmth swells in my chest. I love that she shared her passion with her family, especially her mom. "And you never wanted to go to culinary school? I'm sure you could have." It's true. She has great instincts and the passion for it, which are key in this difficult line of work.

She looks down, and I wonder if I shouldn't have asked. "I was going to, but my mom got sick when I was fourteen, and I moved from cooking to eating. Cooking reminded me too much of her, and eating was a comfort."

"Food has a way of doing that," I say with a warm smile. "But believe me, there's something extremely cathartic in cooking too."

Her eyes land on mine for a second. "Yeah, you might be right."

The waiter interrupts us to ask us if we need anything else, but we're both stuffed. So, we stop by the kitchen to greet Ludovic, our chef for the night. I met him a few years ago at a food festival in the city.

"Ludo," I say, shaking his hand. His kitchen looks just like every other large restaurant's kitchen—Inox and tile everywhere—and I immediately feel right at home. The warm, almost stuffy smell of dish soap as the dishwashers hum in the background, cleaning the day's wares, provides a sense of safety. Yeah, I might be a junkie for dish soap.

"*Ça va?*" he says as his eyes rake Hazel's body. I want to crush his hand when I shake it, but I don't. He really needs his hand. And I could compromise mine.

"*Oui, merci. Je te présente Hazel,* my American friend." No need to pretend here. Unfortunately.

Hazel peers at me, then Ludovic, and he kisses her hand like the gentleman he is. "*Ravi de vous rencontrer.*"

Her blush is on full display as she replies, "*Enchanté.* Sorry for my French, but I just wanted to say your cooking was amazing. I *particularly* loved the duck. Perfectly executed, with so much flavor and tenderness."

"Oh," Ludo says, glancing at me. "I like her." He then directs his attention back to Hazel. "You should eat here more often."

She chuckles, and I force myself to join in, but it sounds more like a growl. "*Oui, c'était délicieux, Ludo. Comme toujours. Merci.*"

"My pleasure."

I clasp my hands together and turn to Hazel. "Great. Should we get going?"

"Sounds good." She casts Ludo one last smile. "Thank you again, so much. I had a fantastic time."

"Thank you for coming, and if you ever visit Paris again, please give me a call."

I press my lips together in an attempt to hold my tongue. Who knows what I might say when he's ogling Hazel that way?

The pink of her cheeks deepens. "I will."

"Bye," I say a little louder, walking away and hoping that Hazel is following. Thankfully, she is.

What was I thinking, taking her to Ludo's restaurant? He's a great guy and an excellent cook. *Wake up, Olivier. You weren't thinking anything. She's not your girlfriend.*

"I did have a great night," she repeats as we're walking down the stairs onto the street. "Thank you again for scoring us a table. And it was so nice of him to invite us to dine, his treat. I mean, that was a very expensive meal. I kind of felt weird accepting it."

I shove my hands in my coat pockets. "Don't. It's what we do between us chefs. It's normal."

"Okay, well, this fake dating thing is really working in my favor," she jokes.

I squeeze my gloves in my pockets. "Yeah. I guess we're both gaining something after all."

And *I'm* starting to think I'll be the one who loses the most.

Chapter 13

Hazel

I have officially landed in heaven. Again. The farmer's market near Olivier's house is my new favorite place on the planet. It's Paris—France—at its finest. Dozens upon dozens of stalls featuring the best locally sourced products, from veggies and fruits to fish, meat, poultry, and delicacies like foie gras. And of course, cheese. I don't have to tell you which stall is my favorite. This is only my second time here, and Pierre, the cheese maker, is already running out of things to have me try. Olivier left me here for half an hour so he could pick up the rest of his ingredients, and I'm not mad about it.

When he returns to the stall, his two tote bags are about to explode.

"Whoa," I say when my wide eyes land on the bags. I'm finishing a piece of Soumaintrain cheese, a creamy and soft variety that tastes both sweet and salty. Go try it if you can; you'll thank me later. "It's delicious, Pierre," I gush before turning to Olivier. "Exactly how many people are we feeding today?"

"About a thousand."

I almost choke on the last bit of cheese. "What?"

He belts out a laugh. "I'm going to test a few different dishes for the festival, so it'll be a lot more intense than yesterday. I'm doing the savory part today and sweet tomorrow."

"Oh! Fun."

"It's a lot of work, though. I don't want you to feel obligated to help. I'm sure you'd rather do something else with your extended stay in Paris, especially as a historian, with your boss calling and everything. I'd hate to get you in trouble."

Crap. "Oh, I've already seen everything I wanted to see. Plus, French food is just as much a part of French history as the architecture. And don't worry about my boss. I sent him everything I needed to earlier," I lie. After meeting Ludo in person, it feels awkward to write his review, so I'm holding off for a few days until I figure out what to write.

"All right. That works for me. You were a great sous chef yesterday."

I offer him my best military salute. "Sous chef Hazel, reporting for duty."

"At ease, soldier," he jests. After we thank Pierre again and bid him goodbye, we begin the walk back to Olivier's house. The weather is pleasant today, a warm fifty-six degrees, and the sun is shining, which gives the small market a tranquil atmosphere. The scene all comes together with a pretty orange backdrop thanks to the trees shedding their leaves around the square.

"What are we going to do with all that food after we test the recipes, though? I don't mind cooking it, and I love eating—look at me," I joke. "But I'm pretty sure there'll be leftovers."

He shakes his head. "We're not going to eat it all. There's a local homeless shelter about ten minutes away. I usually bring any extra food over when I'm testing dishes."

Of course he does. Because he's shown me how generous and selfless he is from day one. Far from the rude, selfish cliché of Parisians we always hear, but he could be the exception to the rule.

Back at the house, we don't waste any time getting to work. I'm on cutting duty—mostly mushrooms and herbs—and Olivier is . . . *now taking off his sweater!* A wave of stifling heat overwhelms me, and it's not because of the oven, where the butternut squashes are currently roasting.

My eyes bulge as I steal a peek at his abs. "What are you doing?"

"Making myself more comfortable," he says casually, stopping mid-pull, as if he's not currently displaying bare skin to me. Sculpted bare skin that I may or may not have tried to envision prior to this. He tugs down the white T-shirt he's wearing underneath, only removing his gray sweater.

Phew! For a second there, I thought the man liked cooking shirtless. Is the clenching of your heart a normal reaction when you're relieved? Because that's what's happening right now. Call me crazy, but it almost feels more like disappointment.

I shake my head, bringing my mind back into focus. No, it's a *relief*. If he cooked shirtless, we'd have a serious problem because this kitchen would be effectively on fire.

"I'm going to make gnocchi," he says in a casual tone, as if his display of skin didn't start a heated monologue in my brain. He takes the butternuts out of the oven, and the warm, honeyed aroma brings me back to reality. The squashes appear crispy and tender at the same time, and my stomach growls instantly.

"Wait." I scrunch my face in confusion, registering what he just said. "Gnocchi from scratch?"

"Yes, of course," he says, as if crafting homemade dumplings is just a part of everyday life.

"Can you teach me?"

He cocks his head to the side and pauses. Maybe he's trying to find a nice way to tell me I'm the sous chef and I need to cut the veggies.

"I'd love to." His bright smile puts his dimple on full display. "We just need to let the squash cool for a few minutes, then we'll remove their skins."

I feel like the butternut squashes aren't the only ones who need to cool down for a few minutes. But then again, talking about removing skin isn't helping.

Once everyone is chill—kinda—he turns the pulp into a puree, then asks me to flour the counter.

"Okay, now for the fun part. Time to get our hands dirty," he says with a lopsided grin.

Am I going to survive this cooking lesson?

Taking the ball of dough, he places it on the counter. "Now, we make a little hole in the middle. In France, we say '*un puits*.'"

"*Un puits*," I repeat. "What does that mean?"

"Um. A place below ground where you can find water?"

"A well?"

"Probably," he says with a smile.

I make a well in the dough, and he places some egg yolks in it along with more flour.

"Now, you just have to knead."

With a firm nod, I place my hands on the smooth dough and start kneading, the egg sticking to my hands. Yeah, I'm not very good at this. "Sorry," I mumble, glancing at him.

"You just need to put a little more passion into it, that's all. More pressure."

I knead with more fervor, and the ingredients start to blend better. He adds more flour, some spices, and a dash of salt. My pace slows down.

"I'm sorry. I suck at this. I hope your sous chef at work is better than me," I joke. "Maybe you should call them up."

"You're fine. You're all I *knead*."

Pausing, I glance toward him. "Did you just make a cooking pun?"

He scratches his forehead, dusting some flour on his eyebrow in the process. "Maybe. Did it work, or am I just pronouncing 'knead' wrong?"

"Nope, you got it right," I say with a giggle. "Good one."

"That's no reason to slack, now. Keep up the pace," he says. "It's the most important part of the process. We need a smooth dough."

He places his hands over mine, and the temperature rises further. He adds so much more pressure, I feel like my hands are going to be kneaded right into the butternut.

"There we go," he says, but when I glance at him, his eyes are fixed on me and not on the dough.

Swallowing, I lower my gaze to my hands. "Is that good?"

"Yes, I think so."

I take a step back. He presses the dough expertly to get it exactly the way he likes it, and I'm in awe of his technique. It's fast, precise, and efficient.

"It looks great. Now, we'll divide it into small balls," he says, separating the dough as he speaks. He hands me one of the balls. "Then, we're going to roll them into logs."

I watch him do the first one and imitate his movements. "Like that?"

"Yep. After that, we cut small pieces, and voilà. We made gnocchi."

"That's it?" I say, my mouth agape at the simplicity of it all.

"Yes, or should I say, 'that's a *wrap*.'" He waggles his eyebrows, making me crack up with laughter. I've always been unable to resist a man who makes jokes. And don't even get me started on puns. They're funny *and* creative. Not to mention hard to come up with when you're speaking a foreign language.

"Darn . . . You're on a *roll* today."

"A cinnamon roll," he adds, puffing with laughter. I'm cackling so hard, I can't even catch my breath.

I place a hand on my aching ribs. "You're killing me."

"Oh, I have a joke," he says. "What do you call a fake noodle?"

"I don't know." I shrug between loud bursts of giggles.

A goofy smile spreads across his face. "An *impasta*."

After gathering my composure, I shake my head. "What a *lime* joke."

He presses his hand over his chest, looking falsely offended. "How dare you! I'm such a *funghi*."

And we keep it going the entire day, one bad cooking pun after the other. Who knew the cooking part could be as fun as the eating part? Or maybe it's just us.

What can I say? We're a couple of *weird-doughs*.

Chapter 14

Olivier

Cooking has always been my passion. It started when I was five, getting my little hands full of flour in my parents' kitchen, and I never stopped. But cooking today with Hazel? That was different. It was *fun*. Pure and simple. Those hours reminded me so much of the first times I stepped foot in a kitchen as a kid, making a mess of everything. Back then, what mattered was the act of cooking. The joy of spending time with my dad or my mom making all sorts of goodies. Of course, eating it was the cherry on top, but I've always wanted to be the one behind the stove.

As I grew up and went to school, then started working, the dynamic shifted. Today, there's so much at stake. People to please, groundbreaking ideas to discover. I always have to be at the top of my game as I chase Michelin stars. But today with Hazel, I wasn't thinking about techniques or what I could add to turn a good dish into a mind-blowing masterpiece. We just cooked. And that felt incredible.

We ended up making only three dishes, but I don't mind. We still have two prep days before the festival. Plus, I needed this.

After dropping off the day's cooking at the shelter, we went into town. Tonight, we're eating at my friend Gabriel's restaurant near the Champs-Elysées, and he reserved us his best, most intimate table that's set in a little alcove.

Hazel looks stunning as always in a simple black dress that showcases her luscious curves.

"The menu looks great," she says, putting it down. "After the deliciousness we made today, I didn't think I'd be hungry, but I underestimated my appetite. My mouth is already watering."

"You don't need to be hungry to enjoy a fine-dining restaurant. Gabriel's cooking is like art," I reply, adjusting my napkin on my knees. "It's more than a meal, it's a treat."

She giggles. "Now, I'm even more excited. So, you and Gabriel went to school together?"

"We did," I say, taking a sip of my champagne. We're doing a champagne-pairing dinner tonight, my favorite. "His dad was great friends with mine, so we met when we were young kids. Later on, we went to cooking school together. We even worked together in Tokyo for a few months."

"That's wonderful. His dad is a chef too?"

A chill creeps up my spine, like it does whenever I think about Marcel. I nod weakly. "Yes. He was one of the greats, but being a chef isn't always easy . . . When he lost one of his stars, he took his own life."

"Oh my," she says, a hand over her mouth. "I'm so sorry. That's awful."

Her hand settles on mine, and I close my eyes. "The dark side of high gastronomy, and why some chefs don't even want to gain a star in the first place. Being awarded one feels great, the biggest accomplishment, but when you lose one . . ."

She squeezes my hand. "Yeah, I can imagine."

"And when the restaurant you work for loses a star right after you arrive, that's even worse." I release a heavy breath. "It means you weren't able to maintain the standards set by your predecessor. There's no greater demise."

She furrows her brows. "Wait. The stars are given to the restaurants and not the chef."

"Right, but every restaurant is reevaluated every year, so it doesn't matter if the chef leaves."

"Talk about pressure," she says, leaning back in her chair.

"And that's just Michelin. There are other organizations who give us ranks and grades—in France and around the world. Basically, we're being judged all day, every day. And if the critic happens to come to the restaurant on a bad day, you're screwed. Bad days are not acceptable in gastronomy."

She swallows hard, looking away. "That's harsh."

"It is. But I understand. Guests come to our restaurants with certain expectations. Having these prestigious stars and grades makes our reputation, so it doesn't matter if someone comes on a bad day. They should have the same experience everyone else had."

"Is it the same in the other countries you've worked in?"

"Yes and no. Food is at the heart of French culture, and the competition is fierce with so many decorated restaurants here. I also feel they might be a little tougher on us here," I say with a weak chuckle. "I guess I'll know soon enough."

Her eyes soften. "You're scared of losing a star. You have three, right?"

"Yes, the restaurant does. My dad earned them over the years, and he never lost one during his tenure. Hopefully, the guide came early in the year when my dad was still there. Even if he was starting to decline, his odds would have been better than mine," I say, bile rising in my throat.

She tilts her head to the side. "Oh, come on. You're a fantastic cook."

"That's not what you said in my restaurant," I half-joke and instantly regret it. Now, my insecurities are on full display, and I don't want her to feel like she has to compliment me to make me feel better.

She blushes until her cheeks are the same shade as her pink lipstick. "You've been cooking for me for days. I'm pretty sure I can attest to your talent, but why not try some of those dishes for the restaurant? Sure, it wasn't high gastronomy, but there were some great ideas there."

"Ah," I say, forcing a smile. "You've hit the touchy subject. I might be the chef of the kitchen, but I'm not the boss, and there's a tremendous difference. I work in a palace, and palace guests have certain expectations. My boss asked me to follow my dad's recipes for each season to the letter."

She shakes her head. "But why hire you if they just wanted someone to execute the old recipes?"

"My guess is the name I bring to the restaurant. I might be wrong, but it feels like that was the driving factor."

"Oh." She wrinkles her forehead. "But I'm sure if you showed your boss what you're capable of, he'd give you a chance to express yourself."

A loud sigh escapes my chest. "I already tried that. He doesn't care about my cooking. All he wants is plain execution to ensure we keep our standing, but I know we won't, because cuisine without passion doesn't win awards."

"How can he be so closed minded? Doesn't he see that a stance like that is bad for the restaurant?"

I stiffen in my chair. "I'm not sure why he's like that. I'll keep trying, though. Maybe with time, things will change." I trail off on my last words.

"You should open your own restaurant," Hazel suggests, clasping her hands. "That way, you're the boss *and* the chef."

I offer a side grin. "Oh, yeah. Easy peasy, right?"

"It doesn't have to be hard. Sure, the administrative part won't be a breeze—I don't think it is in any country—but think of what you could do. You have so many great ideas, and you're passionate about your work. You're incredible, Olivier. People should have the chance to know that."

Her eyes sparkle when they meet mine, and I'm drawn into a surge of emotion.

My heart leaps at her genuine confidence. "Do you really think so?"

She places her hand over mine. "Of course I do."

Never before has someone believed in me like this. Especially not a new acquaintance who's eaten only a few of my regular meals. A picture forms in my brain. Hazel and me standing in front of my new restaurant, full of joy.

Our eyes meet, and I turn my hand over to hold hers. Tingles envelop my heart as the picture becomes clearer in my head. I'm so happy. *We're* so happy. She's smiling from ear to ear and—

Clearing her throat, she removes her hand and takes a sip of water. Just like that, the picture fades.

Swallowing, I look down and pick at my napkin. "I can't. It's just too much, and I'm not ready. Plus, I can't do that to my dad. He retired knowing I would be there to take over. I can't hand his legacy over to someone else."

"Even if staying there makes you unhappy?"

I remain silent.

"Your dad would understand, Olivier. You have real talent. You should showcase it, not hide behind your dad's legacy. Plus, as you said, the customers can feel the lack of passion. So in the end, it's a lose-lose for everyone."

It all sounds so easy and rational. I know she's right, and I'd be lying if I said I didn't think about it myself. "Maybe one day," I rush out in a curt voice. "Right now, I just want to focus on the festival."

Chapter 15

Olivier

I think I'm falling hard for Hazel. Scratch that—I *know* I am. She's kind, funny, loves food as much as I do, and even laughs at my dumb jokes. Not to mention she's beautiful and has a way of making my heart pound every time she looks at me.

She talked so passionately about my job, my future, that it messed with my head. I thought about it all night. Could she be interested in *me* too? I looked for signs when we were cooking earlier, but I didn't get any clear indication that she sees me as more than a friend.

We've finished eating, and we're at the sink doing the dishes when her phone rings somewhere in the room.

"Oh, shoot," she says, drying her hands. "It's probably my sister. I'll be right back."

She darts to the couch, where the sound is coming from, and picks up.

"Hey, Ivy. What's up?" she says, smiling into the screen. Looks like they're video chatting. As they dive into conversation, she walks to her bedroom, shutting the door behind her.

In the meantime, I finish the dishes and start preparing the food containers to bring to the shelter. I'm looking for an extra tote bag at the entryway when I overhear Hazel's voice.

"I miss you too," she says. "I can't wait to get home either, but it's better here now. I'm actually starting to like it."

She stops, Ivy probably having cut her off.

"No, I'm still not taking the job. My life is in the States. I didn't—um—fall in love with the city like you said I would. Anyway." Her words are followed by some noise.

Sensing she might be coming out of her room, I hurry back to the kitchen. My heart is hammering wildly, not because of the roughly sixteen feet I just sprinted, but because Hazel is really going to leave. After our conversation yesterday, I thought something had changed. I also thought I felt something when we were making gnocchi together. Something heavier. A sense of attraction. And then, we laughed so hard . . . Maybe it was just me.

Still, it's been a long time since I've felt this for a woman. I still have a few days left with her, and I have to make the most of every minute. More importantly, I have to make her fall in love with Paris. If I did, maybe she'd have a reason to stay.

"So," I begin when she steps out of her room. "I was thinking we could go into town this afternoon. It's a nice day. Maybe I could show you some of my favorite spots in Paris."

Yep, I'm that smooth.

She leans against the doorframe. "Oh, you don't have to do that. I told you, I've seen plenty already."

My eyebrows shoot up. "And you hated it."

"I don't hate it," she says with a shy smile. "I just don't *love* it. Not the same thing."

I give her a pointed look.

"Anyway, I'm sure you have better stuff to do on your only week off in . . . forever."

"As I said, they're my favorite places. Plus, as a Parisian, I can't let you go back to America with a bad impression of our city. Clichés aren't always true, as you know, but Paris is a wonderful city. You just have to see it from the right angle *and* with the right person. It's not a place to be alone."

She shakes her head. "Are you really that offended that I didn't like it?"

"It is my duty to at least *try* to change your mind," I joke. "Honestly, though, I really want you to leave with a good impression. I know it's not ideal being stuck here, but I don't want you to return home with bad memories of your trip."

"I won't," she breathes. "Have bad memories of my trip, I mean." A short silence falls between us. I'm debating how to break it when she beats me to the punch. "But I see what you're saying. We do have a lot more fun together than I had alone my first week here."

"Alors, on y va?"

She smiles. *"Oui."*

Hazel

I may have cast my judgment on Paris a little too early. And too harshly. After taking the train into town, Olivier brought me to the Parc Monceau, AKA the most charming park in Paris. Scratch that—in the entire world. Tourist guides will tell you about the Jardin des Tuileries, the Jardin du Luxembourg, the Jardin des Plantes, or the Champs de Mars. But why on earth don't they talk about Parc Monceau? It's like stepping into a masterpiece by Claude Monet. Nothing is well-trimmed or organized like in other parks I've been to. Here, nature takes over—overgrown bushes, spontaneous flowers, and ivy creeping over the pathways. From this slice of heaven, we don't even hear the car horns and noises of the city, even though we're right in the middle of it.

"It's gorgeous," I say as we stop in front of a round pond bordered by a Roman colonnade that transports you to another time.

"I know." He gazes at me with a smoldering intensity before directing his eyes back to the pond. "Told you

you'd like it. Did you know it's called a naumachia? It's a lake where mock sea battles took place in ancient Rome."

I hang on his every word, appreciating the depth of his knowledge about the park. I'm already imagining a raging sea battle being fought in the pond when his laugh brings me back to reality.

"But I'm sure you already knew that. I forgot who I'm hanging out with."

I force myself to chuckle along. "Well, I never studied Roman history that deeply, so it's fascinating for me."

He opens his mouth, but I'm quicker. I don't want to give him a chance to ask what I studied. "Please, tell me more," I say. "How did it end up here in Paris? And I'm pretty sure it's not a real naumachia. Those had to have been massive since they held entire ship fights."

My heart is pounding now, and I pray I didn't just stick my foot in my mouth.

"Right. In the eighteenth century, this was the Duc of Chartres' garden. He was a bit of a megalomaniac and asked a famous painter to envision a sumptuous bucolic garden with rivers, minarets, mills, this naumachia, and even Egyptian tombs. It was like a world tour."

"Wow," I breathe quietly, truly in awe as I look around me.

"The garden was eventually seized during the revolution, and it was pretty much completely forgotten. About one hundred years later, Napoleon III decided to restore it. It's a lot smaller than it used to be, though."

"This place is amazing. How do you know so much about the garden? Are you a historian as well as a chef?"

Smiling, he glances back at the naumachia. "Definitely not. But I love this place, and there are so many oddities here that I just had to dig deeper and understand. Do you want to see the rest of it? We can check out the pyramid if you want."

"Sure."

We continue our exploration of the garden, and I feel like the only words coming out of my mouth are "oh," "wow," and "beautiful." Most of the trees have already shed their leaves, which has created a carpet of yellow and orange on the ground. With the sun casting its rays over the park, the crisp leaves turn to gold.

We pass several sculptures, a bridge, an old-style carousel, a few small waterfalls, and the famous pyramid. Parisians are relaxing on benches, talking or reading while others are walking their dogs or enjoying a romantic stroll together. It's so peaceful, I could stay here forever. I get why they try not to advertise it too much.

We're now walking to a narrower, more private part of the park, and on every bench—literally—couples are cuddled up, kissing or hugging. A lump forms in my throat as I fight with my infuriating imagination, which is picturing Olivier and me cuddling on one of these benches. Not going to happen.

"So, are you falling in love?" he asks just before we exit the park.

My eyes widen. "What?"

"With Paris," he says, as if that should have been obvious. "How did you like our first stop?"

"Oh, right. Yes, I loved it. This place is truly magical. Where are we going next?"

"To a small village inside the city—Montmartre. I know you've probably been there already, but I want to bring you to my favorite corners of it."

"I didn't, actually. I spent most of my time in museums for my, um, research."

Surprise flashes across his face, giving way to a smile. "You're going to love it."

We walk for about thirty minutes before finally ending up in the quaint streets of Montmartre. I've heard about this neighborhood, of course—specifically its basilica—and it looks like I'm not the only one. There are many more tourists bustling through here than at the park, but if Olivier brought me here, he must have his reasons.

The cobbled streets are undoubtedly charming, and I get why he called it a village. Once again, I feel like we've been transported outside the French capital. Cafés and street artists line the paths, offering to paint your portrait or playing their accordions. *Finally.* That's where they've been hiding. The accordion playing in Paris is a real thing after all. I just didn't know where to look.

Not wanting to look too clueless, I take advantage of a restroom break to have a look online so I know at least a bit about this place. And if it explodes my phone bill, so be it. I need a lifeline here.

When I emerge from the restrooms, he shows me another, smaller park lush with nature. We also visit an unexpected vineyard right on the butte of Montmartre, a windmill, and Le Mur Des Je T'aime, a large wall where the words "I love you" are written in every language in the world. Naturally, it's another popular place for couples.

"Should we stop and have something to eat?" he asks. "There's a cute *crêperie* at the corner. Walking up all those steps made me hungry." He taps his stomach, and I can only agree. I've loved wandering around Montmartre, but those stairs are no joke.

"Well, I never say no to crêpes," I answer with a smile.

Making our way to the eatery, we sit down at a table outside. Fifteen minutes later, we're enjoying our crêpes with a cup of coffee.

"So, what's the verdict?" Olivier inquires after taking a bite. "There is so much more to explore, but we'd need a lifetime to see it all."

"I loved it. It's very different from the Paris I saw by myself. Which was a lot more"—I rub my chin—"urban, I guess."

"Yes, that makes sense. When you come here, you want to see all the touristic places and museums, but Paris isn't really a city that you visit. At least, not if you really want to get to know the city, discover it. You have to take your time, wander, get lost. That's when you truly see Paris."

"Yeah," I say, taking a bite of my Grand Marnier crêpe. "I see what you mean. And there was even some accordion music, so I'm good."

He tilts his head back in a laugh. "Well, there you go. At least Hollywood didn't make that one up."

"Isn't it a little sad to live here alone sometimes, though? As you said, Paris is better experienced with someone else, and I can clearly see that." I glance around at all the couples at the tables around us.

He scratches his trim beard. "It can be. But you can feel lonely anywhere. Paris isn't unique in that way. If anything, it might be even easier to find love here because of the romantic vibe."

I quirk an eyebrow. "Says the guy who needed me as a fake date."

He rolls his eyes. "Ah, come on. We've been over this, Hazel. I'm just saying, if you're looking for *love* in Paris, you'll find it."

"Fine. Maybe you're right," I joke. "But I usually don't have trouble finding love. It's keeping it that's the problem."

"Really? Why's that?" he asks, his question surprising me. He's perfectly casual about it. No intensity in his eyes or tension in his shoulders, like the rigor that's seizing my entire body.

"Oh," I say, twirling my *café au lait*. "Well, if I had the answer, we wouldn't be having this conversation." I chuckle. "I guess it's not my season of love or whatever. I know, it's cheesy."

"*Non*. I get it. We all go through different seasons in life."

I tilt my head to the side. Could a man actually understand the concept? They must be made different here in France. "Yeah. And I really tried after my last breakup. It's actually embarrassing how hard I tried. We're talking blind dates, speed dates, online dates, double dates. I did it all in an attempt to forget my ex."

"Did it work? Did you forget him?" he asks in a breath.

I nod slowly. "I did. Not because of the many, *many* bad dates I suffered through, but because I realized he wasn't good for me. He didn't love me. He kept trying to change who I am, like getting me to follow some crazy weight loss routine or eat kale or whatever," I say with a chuckle.

He arches an eyebrow. "What do you have against kale?"

I wrinkle my nose in disgust. "Not very tasty."

"Oh, but it can be," he says. "Every vegetable can. You just have to know how to cook it."

"Well, my ex just pulverized it in smoothies and called that lunch."

His expression of disgust mirrors mine. "Yikes."

"Told you. Like I said, he wasn't good for me."

"Definitely not," he says, shaking his head vehemently. "Well, let's go. I just got inspired."

"Where are we going?" I ask, getting up after him.

He drops some money on the table. "We need to get to the market before it closes, and then we're going home. I'm going to cook you kale tonight, and you're going to love it."

I have no doubt about that. Olivier has a gift of making everything taste like it was touched by the gods.

Chapter 16

Hazel

I rescind every bad thing I ever said about Kale. This stuff is good. It might even be my new favorite green after last night. You might think I'm crazy, but if you had Olivier cook you a *poêlée d'escargots* with chorizo butter, butternut, and kale for dinner, you'd love it too. Snails are actually delicious—even if the texture is a little squishy—and coupled with the crisp appeal of the chorizo, the roundness of the butter and creamy squash, and the earthy, green notes of the kale, it was the perfect autumn dish.

We barely finished breakfast two hours ago, and we're already leaving for the restaurant. It's true what they say about the French—eating is a big part of their lives, and I'm here for it. But with the small lump that has lodged in my stomach, I'm not sure I'll be able to enjoy the meal much. Tonight is Joelle's Halloween party, and I'm equal parts excited and nervous. There will be a lot more people there, which means more eyes on Olivier and me. Which also means we'll have to step into our acting roles a bit more. Is it weird to admit that's the part I'm excited about?

And the food. That is, if I'm able to eat it.

We use the metro again to reach the city center. It's definitely not my favorite means of transport. The train cars are gloomy, dirty, and smell like piss, but the part where Olivier and I have to squeeze against each other isn't so bad.

"Do you know the chef this time?" I ask as we stroll down the street to the restaurant.

"I do. How do you think I managed to score us a table?" He winks. "Most of these restaurants are booked for weeks, if not months, in advance."

"Don't I know it." I force a tight smile. Great. I should have known better. Every place he's taking me to will be friends of his. How on earth am I supposed to review them now?

The restaurant is the epitome of Parisian chic, with dark-green velvet draped on the walls, the luxury enhanced with shimmering golden fixtures and leather seats. A young man in a suit guides us to our table, which has been set up in a cozy private room. This is something I could definitely get used to.

"Thank you again," I say once we've ordered, "for making this happen. I feel so lucky to have the chance to try so many restaurants within such a short time frame." As a foodie, I really do. As a food critic who's supposed to be working—but can't—I hate it.

"You did great on your own your first week here," he says with a chuckle.

I lay my napkin on my lap. "True, but I'd been planning it for weeks."

"The schedule of a chef can be hectic, so we always do our best to accommodate a colleague. It's as much a treat for me as it is for you. I don't get much time off to eat out, and dining alone is definitely not the same."

"Yeah, so true."

"But you were eating alone when we met."

I grimace. "I wasn't about to miss out on Paris' amazing food just because I was here alone. I'd rather eat in solitude than not enjoy the city's offerings, you know?"

He gives me a nod. "Agreed."

"Let's drink to that," I say, raising my glass of water.

"*Non.*" He pulls his glass away. "We don't toast with water. It's bad luck."

My eyes flash wide open. "Oh! I didn't know that. Sorry. Any other French food superstitions I should know about? I wouldn't want to commit a faux pas tonight."

"Are you nervous about the party?" he asks, tilting his head. "We don't have to go, you know."

I swat him softly. "Of course we're going. We told your mom. But yeah, I guess I am a teensy bit nervous. A party is always intimidating."

He averts his eyes for a second. "It might be, but I promise I'll stay with you the whole time. Just ignore everything my mom says, and it'll be fine."

I nod. Yeah, it's going to be fine. Olivier will be there.

"And as for food superstitions, we have *a lot of them*," he declares with a goofy smile. "The most famous is that you should never put the baguette, or the bread, upside down on the table because it symbolizes death. When clinking glasses, we must look into each other's eyes, or we'll endure seven years of bad love. Also, we may never cross the glasses—if we're more than two, obviously—because it brings bad luck. And on the same note, you shouldn't cross your fork and knives on the table. That brings conflict. I could go on and on."

I blink back. "Oh, my. There are a lot of rules. Mostly about not crossing things."

"Yep."

"In the States, we have a few too. Like never spill salt on the table because it brings misfortune, or never gift someone a knife because it brings discord in the relationship. Never seat thirteen at a table because it's bad luck . . ."

"We have those as well," he says with a nod. "I was only joking, though. I don't take those superstitions too seriously. Otherwise, there isn't a lot left that you can do."

"I sure hope not," I say with a giggle.

"Except the 'looking each other in the eye when toasting.' That one I can't shake."

I arch my eyebrows. "Not ready to risk seven years of bad love, huh?"

His eyes crinkle under his smile. "Absolutely not. The 'no love' thing is already plenty for me."

"Now that you mention it, I've been racking my brain trying to think whether I forgot to look someone in the eye while toasting a while back," I say, scratching my chin. "If I did, hopefully I'm reaching the end of the period. Do the years add up if you do it again?"

His deep chuckle booms across the table. "No idea. But I'm sure you can find extensive guides online."

"Gosh, I hope that's not the case, or I'll stay single my entire life."

His deep eyes plunge into mine. "I don't believe that for a second."

The air suddenly becomes stuffy, and I refrain from fanning myself with my palm. Thankfully, the waiter interrupts us to bring us bread, followed by the first dish. He takes his time explaining it to us.

I'm immediately impressed by the presentation. It's very elegant, with touches of color around the plate. The whole thing looks like a work of art.

"Wow."

"Yep. Leon is an artist," Olivier says. "And the best part—it's as delicious as it looks."

Every dish is more beautiful than the last, and we're having a great time. We talk about cultural differences between France and the USA, diving into even more superstitions. It turns out that most of them are universal.

We're now eating the first dessert, a maple syrup pecan pie, and it's a succulent choice. This is the first time I've eaten an American dish in France, and I must say, Leon did it right. It truly tastes like home. Eager to eat more, I shove a large piece into my mouth, but it stays stuck in my trachea. I struggle to make it go down, but it sticks to the back of my throat. I grab some water, but it doesn't go through. Then, I try to spit it out, but the offending morsel doesn't budge.

I start to sweat, my heart rattling in my ribcage as I realize with a wave of dread what's happening. I'm choking.

Olivier

Panic courses through my body as Hazel grows paler. "*Mon dieu. Hazel, ça va?*" She looks like she's choking.

Flying up from my chair, I slap my hand twice on her back, trying to clear her throat. I look at her, but her eyes are now bulging, and she's gesturing frantically to her throat. She can't breathe.

I step behind her and lift her up, wrapping my arms around her to perform the Heimlich maneuver, just like I learned in culinary school. I apply a strong pressure to her stomach, but it doesn't work. My hands are trembling, and my arms are weak. This is not happening. *Come on, Olivier. Focus.* I suck in a quick breath, trying to chase away the worst-case scenario plaguing my mind. I go in again, this time with a burst of strength, and the pecan pie bite shoots across the room. Hazel falls back against me, and I let out a loud breath of relief. My heart is still pounding, and though I know I should, I can't let go of her. *Merci mon dieu.* I've only known Hazel for a week, but a world without her is inconceivable. It'd be like living in darkness.

"Are you okay?" I ask, rubbing her arms.

Placing a hand on her chest, she inhales a deep breath. "Yes. I think so."

"Are you sure?" I spin her around gently, caressing her cheek. We lock eyes for a minute, and my heart swells with relief when I see a shade of pink in my finger trail. Fire blazes in my eyes, and I'm inches away from kissing her.

"Positive," she says. She sits back down, her chest still heaving rapidly, the rise and fall matching my own.

My heart hammers so hard against my chest, I think I'm going to be the one who needs saving soon.

I pour more water in her glass, and she drinks a few sips before smiling. "Thank you for saving me."

"Of course," I say, leaning back against my chair and taking a deep breath.

"It was kind of a big *dill*," she says, glancing up at me with a grin. "Get it? A big 'dill'?"

As I shake my head, a smile spreads across my face, calming my racing heart. "Now I know you're okay if you're making such lame food puns."

She laughs, and my breathing finally slows. "Well, come on, then. Show me what you've got." She crosses her arms over her chest.

"Girl, *peas*. I'm not about to *leek* all my secrets to you just yet," I say, arching my eyebrows.

Her mouth opens slightly, then she bites her lower lip. My heart picks up its pace again.

Gentlemen, can I have your attention please? I think I just cracked the code. What if the path to a woman's heart is paved with clever food puns?

"You win," she says, her eyes twinkling with mirth. "I have *muffin* more to say. Thank goodness you were able to *romaine* so calm."

Darn it, this girl is amazing. I could keep this going forever.

Hazel insists that we don't skip the second dessert and the mini pastries before we go thank the chef. Despite the incident, she assures him that she had an amazing time, and I can only agree with her. Which makes me lean toward opening my own restaurant even more. Creative control is key to a fruitful career. But as we chat with my friend, Hazel keeps rubbing her chest, and worry scratches at my mind. What if I hurt her when I did the Heimlich maneuver? I know it should only be done in extreme circumstances when someone isn't able to breathe because you can easily break a rib. Her case certainly fit the bill, but what if I applied too much pressure?

"Are you okay?" I whisper to her as Leon shows us his new state-of-the-art oven.

"Yes, I'm fine," she says with a grin, but I can feel she's lying.

After a few more minutes, we bid goodbye to Leon and the kitchen staff before getting our coats back from the hostess.

As she puts her coat on, Hazel winces. Now I'm beyond worried.

"You're not okay," I say when we reach the street, my heart clenching. "You're hurting. We're going to the hospital, now." Taking her hand, I start walking.

She tugs at my hand to stop me. "Olivier. No, I'm perfectly fine. This is silly."

I stop and swing around to look her in the eye. "You're not fine. I've noticed you rubbing your chest and wincing.

I hurt you." I rake a frustrated hand through my hair. "Gosh. I'm so sorry, Hazel. We'll fix this."

"You did what you had to do. You saved me," she murmurs, her voice soft as she squeezes my hand again.

Our eyes lock, but I can't stand seeing her like this. I can feel her pain. "Either way, we're going to the hospital. There's a good chance I cracked one of your ribs."

She stops arguing, probably noting the distress in my voice, and we make our way to the nearest hospital. Thankfully, there isn't a long wait, and she sees a nurse after a few minutes. It's a good thing they need me to translate because that keeps my mind occupied. My blood pressure is probably alarmingly high right now, and I keep pacing the room like a caged lion.

"Calm down," Hazel soothes as we're waiting for her x-ray results. I can't even look at her. She's perched on the edge of an examination table, wearing a hospital gown because of me. If I hurt her, I will never forgive myself.

"I feel fine," she continues. "I'm sure it's nothing."

I don't answer, aware that she's only saying those things to make me feel better. Instead, I continue pacing, which helps with my stuttering heart.

"Good news," the doctor says as he glides into the room. "There's no cracked rib."

A long swoosh of air escapes my lungs, and I clutch my stomach. "*Merci, Docteur.* But why is she hurting, then? Is that normal?" I ask, my panic rising again. Perhaps they missed something.

"I'm fine, Olivier," Hazel says in a comforting tone.

"She is," the doctor agrees with an empathetic smile. "It's probably just from the pressure of your fists. You did good, though—probably saved her life. The pain will subside in a day or two."

As I bob my head, I let his words sink in. "Thank you," I say, shaking the doctor's hand. As soon as he's gone, I slump into a chair, relieved. A few seconds later, Hazel rests her hands on my shoulders.

"I told you I was fine. You did nothing wrong, Olivier. You saved me. Thank you again." Then, she kisses my cheek, effectively setting it on fire. I'm so dazzled by that kiss, I don't even realize she put her coat back on.

"Should we get going? We have costumes to buy."

"What?" I raise my head, meeting her gaze. "We don't have to go to the party. We had enough emotion for one day." Plus, my mom's parties are always an excuse for her to meddle even further in my personal life. Her seeing Hazel twice within such a short period is going to put false ideas into her head. And mine.

"Olivier, don't use this as an excuse to ditch your mom's party," she scolds in a tone that reminds me of my mom. "We said we'd be there, so we're going." Her eyes twinkle. "Plus, shopping for costumes is always fun."

Chapter 17

Hazel

I have to assure Olivier I'm perfectly fine a few times—using bad food puns—before he actually believes me. It was sweet, and even a little sexy, the way he worked himself into a frenzy with worry for me. His genuine concern brought a flock of butterflies swarming to my belly. Except for the part when I was actually choking. That was terrifying, and the pecan pie expulsion was definitely *not* sexy at all.

We're now browsing a cute *boutique de costumes* to choose what we're wearing tonight. Olivier zooms straight to the back of the store, picks up a headband with devil's horns, plus another one with a witch's hat and a spider brooch, before booking it back to the cashiers.

"What are you doing?" I ask with a frown.

"This will do fine," he says, shaking the items in his hands for emphasis. "We don't need to go over the top. It's just my mom's party. Frankly, I usually don't even dress up. I just say I have a chef costume, and everyone laughs."

I cock my head to the side, steeling my expression. "Well, not this time, mister. You're not about to rob me of a Halloween shopping spree in France."

His arms drop to his sides. "Really? This hardly qualifies as shopping."

"It's clothes and accessories. It definitely qualifies."

He hesitates, but then his eyes crinkle with a smile. "Okay. I'm in."

We walk around the store, browsing our options, and I'm surprised to mainly see spooky costumes. Pumpkins, devils, witches, monsters, bats—the list goes on.

"These are only scary costumes," I say, glancing around the store. "I was hoping to go as a baguette or a slice of cheese."

He laughs hard, clutching his stomach. Once he recovers, he says, "It's Halloween. It's supposed to be scary."

"I know, but the costumes aren't always spooky. The last Halloween party I went to, I dressed up as Cher, and my sister was a cowgirl"

His forehead wrinkles. "That's Carnival, not Halloween."

"I guess you're right. Lately, Halloween in the US has just become a reason to dress up as sexy anything. At first it was, like, sexy bloody nurse, sexy cat, or hot witch. But now, people use any excuse to show cleavage and wear a short skirt."

With his eyes fixed on me, he swallows hard. "Oh, well . . ."

"But I like this better. This is what Halloween is all about," I say, picking up a set of fake vampire teeth from the shelf. "Looks like you guys nailed this American tradition."

Joelle and Phillippe's house looks like something right out of a spooky Halloween movie. One step out of the car with the help of my scythe—yes, I am the grim reaper tonight—and I can already tell that Joelle spared no expense. The front yard is scattered with graves, skulls, and skeletons. Large spiders are sitting on the lawn, and carved pumpkins are lit along the path up to the house.

"It looks amazing."

"You know my mom. Always over the top," Olivier says, walking around the car in his vampire costume. I never really understood that sexy vampire thing before, but I sure do now.

He slips his fake teeth in and grabs my hand as we walk to the front door—which bears a wreath made of bones and spiderwebs today. He doesn't bother to ring the bell and opens the door, waving me in before him.

"Hazel! Olivier, *vous voilà!*" Joelle gushes, opening her arms as she sees us. She's wearing a green-and-purple witch costume that makes me think of Winifred Sanderson in *Hocus Pocus*.

"*Bonsoir.*" She plants two kisses on my cheeks, then does the same to her son. "*Tu t'es déguisé! Oh je suis trop contente.*" Then, she turns to me. "First time he comes with costume. Thank you."

I glance at Olivier, who gives me a look that says, "I told you so." We follow Joelle around the house, and I can only marvel at the decorations. Ghosts and scary witches are suspended at every corner, and garlands of bats drape from the ceiling. Carved pumpkins of various sizes glow with flickering candles, and spooky ambiance music serves as the finishing touch to set the mood. Joelle moves through the room, introducing us to some of her friends and family. I have no idea what everyone's names are. They're talking so fast, and the names are hard to pronounce for an American like me. Everyone seems friendly, though.

"Hazel, you look great!" Agathe says, kissing me in greeting. This time, I don't even flinch. I'm getting used to it.

"Thank you. So do you."

She's a witch too, but she looks like a character straight from Harry Potter. Sure enough, Juliette and Camille both bounce up to their mother dressed as Hermione, waving their wands in the air in the most adorable way.

They kiss us both, then start talking at lightspeed to their uncle, showing him their winnings from trick or treating. The way he's so patient and kind with his nieces does weird things to my body, and I need to tear my eyes away. Thankfully, Matt joins us at the same moment, wearing a lifelike costume of the Joker that's downright terrifying.

We mingle for a while before having a chance to sample Joelle's amazing cuisine. As I suspected, she went all out. Everything looks as good as it tastes, but my favorites are the mini pumpkin pies, which are bursting with flavor. The crunched nuts sprinkled on top add an interesting texture, contrasting with the smooth filling. Though I'm also quite fond of the foie gras bats.

"Hazel," Joelle says, finding me again. Olivier just left for the bathroom. "I am so happy to see you again. You remember Eliane, my friend I introduced you to earlier?"

"I do." I smile at Eliane with a nod. "*La nourriture est* fantastic, Joelle," I say.

"Oh, it's nothing, dear. *Merci*," Joelle says with a wave. "Hazel *est* very beautiful, *n'est-ce pas?*" she asks her friend. "*Elle* and Olivier will make very beautiful children."

Good thing I just swallowed my pie, or we'd be having a repeat of the lunch incident. I force a smile while the two women start chatting as if I'm not here. I don't understand everything, but I'm pretty sure they're already naming our children and discussing wedding locations. And the weird thing is, that doesn't make me want to run. No, it actually makes me wish I could understand French perfectly so I could revel in the fantasy they're creating for Olivier and me.

I might be the grim reaper tonight, but there's one thing becoming clearer and clearer by the minute. Olivier has reaped my heart and soul, but I've never felt more alive than when I'm with him. And that's what scares me to death.

Olivier

After a bathroom break, I'm headed back to the living room in search of Hazel when I come across my dad. True to himself, he's not wearing much of a costume. Only a pair of bat's ears.

"*Salut, Papa*," I greet, kissing him on the cheeks. Yes, we do that between men too. But only the ones we're close with. And no, it's not weird. "*Ça va?*"

"*Oui, et toi? Comment se passe le travail?*"

Here we go. We can't exchange more than three words without him bringing work to the table. No pun intended this time.

I wring my hands like a kid about to come clean to his parents. Well, in a way, I am. "It's fine," I tell him. "But I'm not sure it's a good fit for me after all."

His face reddens, and I can practically see his blood pressure rising. "Of course it's a good fit, Olivier. You're a *Brun*. Maybe if you didn't take vacation days so early in your contract, you'd fit right in. That's not how you start a career in a palace."

My blood freezes in my veins, but I can't let this go. I have to tell him. "That's the thing, though. I'm not sure I want to work in palaces anymore. I'm thinking of opening my own restaurant."

"Olivier!" he thunders. "I will not hear a word of it. The Brun family name is synonymous with prestige. My grandfather and I both worked exclusively in palaces our entire careers. There is *nothing* better for you than this."

"I know, but I'm not sure that's my path. Although I have the utmost respect for your work, I would like to create my own imprint on this world. Something that feels more 'me.'"

"Olivier." His voice is calmer, though the fire is still roaring in his eyes. "You've trained all your life for excellence. Stepping down from a palace to open your own restaurant would be a mistake. Don't settle for anything less."

With a shallow sigh, I nod. "*Oui, Papa.*" I should have known. Discussing this with him is a lost cause. We'll never see eye to eye. Still, I have to do what feels right for me. And maybe one day, he'll come around. Maybe he'll eventually stop being so hard-headed, though if I'm being realistic, there's probably a bigger chance of Matt becoming fluent in English than my dad admitting he might have been wrong about something.

In the distance, I see Hazel gazing off, lost deep in her thoughts. I feel bad that I left her to fend for herself this entire time. Then, horror takes over when I see my mom and Eliane chatting her up. I groan. Mom always gets extra when she's with her close friend.

Right on cue, the first word coming out of my mom's mouth when I reach them is "marriage."

"Mom!" I scold, panic rising in my throat. "Stop. *Tu vas la faire fuir.*" Glimpsing Hazel's face, I'd say I'm right about that. She's two steps away from sprinting out of the house.

My mom's hand flies to her mouth. "*Pardon, mon chéri. Juste* one more thing. Hazel, can we *prendre* a picture of us as a memory?" she asks, taking her phone out.

"Oh, *bienne sur*," Hazel says with a sweet grin.

Mom hands me the camera, and I snap a picture of them, my heart constricting in my chest as I realize it's probably the only one I'll ever have.

"You should get in here too," Hazel says, beckoning me to join them.

I ask Eliane to take the picture as I squeeze in between my two favorite women, a huge smile on my face.

"*Et maintenant* one with the two of you," Mom says, getting out of the shot, a hand over her heart.

Hazel and I pose like a couple of teenagers before prom when my brother shouts, "Kiss her, Oli."

Looks like he's learned two more words in English. I wish he would keep his new education to himself. Well, okay. Maybe I'm just a tiny bit grateful.

I turn to her, and she smiles at me. Closing the distance, we press our lips together, holding the kiss long enough for the picture to be taken.

"Booooo," Matt yells. "*Embrasse la correctement*," he says before whispering something to Agathe, who murmurs something back. He shouts again, "Kiss your girl like you mean it. Don't be shy."

Agathe needs to stop giving him English lessons, *tout de suite*. I can feel Hazel tense up next to me. The last thing I want is to kiss her against her will. Even if there's nothing else I'd rather do than feel her lips on mine.

I turn back to her, wearing a discreet—I hope—frown in an attempt to apologize.

Pressing her lips together, she gives me a little nod, and my mouth dries in anticipation. Yeah, this is going to be one weird French kiss if I don't have any saliva.

Breathe, Olivier.

Tucking her chin in my hand, I bring her closer to me. Her hands fall on my chest, and I wonder if she can feel my pounding heart. Who am I kidding? The entire room probably can. It's beating louder than the creepy ambiance music my mom put on.

    Our lips connect, and I gently part hers with mine. The kiss completely and utterly consumes me. It hammers at the walls I've erected around my heart. Harder and harder, only stopping once it finally breaks through and reaches my heart. Leaving it exposed. Vulnerable.

Chapter 18

Hazel

"I'm sorry again about my mom, and that *kiss*," Olivier says as he pulls up in front of the school and finds a parking spot. The festival is tomorrow, and we're going to spend the day in the school's kitchen cooking and doing prep work.

"Ah, don't worry. Like I said, it's fine."

I gaze out the window to hide my blush. The truth is, it's more than fine. He's welcome to kiss me like that any time he wants. French kissing a Frenchman is completely different than doing it with an American. It's on another level. Earth shattering. Or maybe it's just Olivier?

"I know, but it's not what you signed up for. We said 'kissing with no tongue,' and—well—I didn't want to break the rules."

"No, you're right," I say, forcing the memory away. Yeah, we should stick to the rules. Rules are important. Rules are needed. I clear my throat. "So, are we ready to go?"

He looks at me one more time before opening the car door. "Are you sure you're okay, though? Your ribs? I don't want you to lift stuff and cook all day if--"

I give him a pointed look. "Olivier, you've asked at least a dozen times since yesterday. I'm fine. I don't even feel anything anymore." Okay, it's still a little sore, but it doesn't really hurt.

He sighs. "Sorry. I just hate that I hurt you." He looks down, his mouth twisting.

"You didn't," I say, placing my hand on his forearm. "Now, let's do this."

Nodding, he gives me a feeble smile, and we get out of the car.

We'll be cooking most of the food and completing the preparations today so that we only have to reheat them tomorrow. We narrowed the offerings down to our favorite dishes from what we tested the last few days, and we swung by the market this morning to pick up everything. And let me tell you, there is *a lot* of food.

Just when I'm wondering if we'll manage it all with only four hands, I meet the half dozen members of the Parent-Teacher Association who've offered their help today. All women. All dressed to impress. They're standing in the kitchen in their high heels, tight jeans, and cleavage-heavy blouses, looking at Olivier like he's their favorite snack.

"*Mesdames*," Olivier says, entering behind me with his arms full of cardboard boxes. "*Merci d'être venues aujourd'hui. Nous avons une paire de main supplémentaire,*" he continues, turning to me. "This is my girlfriend, Hazel. She's American, and she's here to help as well."

My heart leaps in my throat when he says the word "girlfriend," even though I knew it was coming. After all, we have to keep up appearances since Olivier's family will be at the festival tomorrow.

"*Bonjour*," I say with a smile and a friendly wave. Some of them answer, but I can hear the hushed whispers of "*Americaine*." And the way they look me up and down.

I knew the French were famous for always being chic, but we'll be cooking all day, so I figured jeans and a light sweater would do the trick.

They each kiss Olivier twice, once on each cheek, putting a hand on his shoulder when they lean in. As they do, I want to rip their hands off. Olivier is dressed casually too, now that I think of it. A blue sweater with black jeans. But he doesn't count. He always looks good.

Embarrassed by my fashion choice, I don't wait for him as I walk back to the car and unload the rest of the goods. Only two other women help.

My much-anticipated day of cooking fun with Olivier quickly turns into a nightmare. He gives us all directions to follow, very clearly. Or at least they are in English. I would think they'd be even clearer in French since it's his first language, but apparently, the women still feel the need to interrupt him every five minutes to ask him to show them something. "How do I make the dressing again, Olivier?" *He explained it five minutes ago in painstaking detail.* "How do you want this chopped,

Olivier?" *He already said, in squares.* "Am I doing this right, Olivier?" *No, you're purposely not.* "Can you help me, Olivier?" *I'm sure he has better things to do.*

I hate this. So much. Because my growing annoyance only showcases the feelings I'm catching for Olivier, and I can't help but feel like I'm being punished for something I did. Or is it karma?

Did I kill a bird and not realize it or something? There must be an explanation for the fact that I'm falling for the hottest, nicest, funniest French man in existence, who kisses like a god, when I live thousands of miles away and he's not looking for a relationship. It doesn't matter how *canon* I may be. He made it perfectly clear he doesn't want a girlfriend, and I believe him. After all, he could have any one of these gorgeous women. One snap of his fingers, and they'd probably be naked in his bed.

Olivier appears next to me, startling me. "*Penne* for your thoughts?"

I'm so annoyed right now with those women and myself, I only respond with a feeble smile.

"Darn," he says, shaking his head. "I hesitated between that and 'pickle.' Should have gone with pickle."

My smile widens. "Penne works better, I think."

"What's up?" He bumps me with his shoulder. "It doesn't look like you're having a *grate* day."

I turn to see the large grin stretching across his face, that irresistible dimple on full display. Then, he waggles his eyebrows, and that does it for me. I explode in laughter.

"Ah, much better," he says. "But seriously, are you okay? You haven't said a word in a while."

"I'm fine," I reply, bobbing my head. "Just focused on making my gnocchi, that's all."

He frowns. "Okay. Well, when you're done, can you show Catherine how to properly fold the ravioli? She's having trouble making them stick. You are my sous chef, after all, and I need to delegate."

The only American in the kitchen giving a cooking lesson to a French woman? I'm sure she's going to love that.

"Me? What are *they,* then?" I gesture to the women with my chin.

"They're commis. You're the most trusted member of my brigade."

"Wow. Okay," I say, wiping my hands with a dish towel. "Right away, chef."

After I show Catherine, twice, how to properly fold the ravioli so they'll stick during the cooking phase, she finally gets it. She wasn't nice, by any means, but she was less awful than I expected considering the way she glared at me earlier, so that's something.

"*So*," she says, drawing out the vowel as I'm about to return to my station. "You and Olivier. Iz it seriousse?"

"Oh, um. It's still very new, so . . ."

"You are a lucky woman. Olivier does not date. At least, that's what he said to me." Her accent is so strong, it could cut a butternut squash in two. But I'm not judging. At least she can produce a coherent sentence in English. More than can be said about me in French.

"Yes, I guess I am," I say as both our gazes are drawn toward him. He's cutting vegetables at lightspeed, and like everything Olivier does in the kitchen, it comes off as extremely sexy. Jacqueline is actually fanning herself, and there's some drool at the corner of Catherine's mouth. I wipe my mouth, just in case I'm in the same state.

"How did you meet 'im?" Catherine asks, focusing back on me.

"At his restaurant. I dined there."

"Oh, I see. So you are a rich American. Maybe that's what it takes to be his girlfriend," she snaps before turning back to her ravioli folding. Okay, so maybe I was right about her the first time.

I jump at the opportunity to get away, escaping back to my station. I sort of understand where Catherine is coming from, though. When there's a nice, funny, hot guy who takes days off to cook food for his nieces' school, you need to find a reason why he's not interested in you. Just to ease your pain. Especially if you're as good looking as Catherine—short blonde bob, wide blue eyes, and porcelain skin. She's gorgeous.

Four hours later, we're finally done. We cooked and arranged everything we could and stored it all for tomorrow's big event.

"Are you coming for drinks tonight?" Catherine asks, addressing Olivier and me as we're saying goodbye in the parking lot.

Drinks? Goodness. I'm exhausted after today, and tomorrow is sure to be even crazier. How do these people do it? I muffle a yawn.

"Actually," Olivier says, casting me a quick glance, "I was thinking we'd skip it, but have fun."

A shadow of disappointment flashes over her face. "But it's our tradition."

"*Pas cette fois*, Catherine," he says with a smile before opening his trunk to pack a box of supplies inside. "*À demain.*"

Wait, is he really refusing a night out with a bunch of women who worship him, just to stay home with me? Not that I'm complaining. A night in with Olivier is my favorite kind of night, but I didn't know he felt the same way. Looks like the butterflies are back in my belly, and this time, there's no stopping them.

"*Oui, à demain,*" she responds. I wave goodbye to her, but she doesn't even glance my way.

"Are you sure you don't want to go out with them?" I ask when we sit down in the car. "I don't want you to miss out because of me."

"Frankly, I'd much rather stay home with you tonight."

My mouth goes dry, and my mind freezes when I try to formulate an answer.

He coughs a little. "I mean, we're getting up so early tomorrow. We have to keep up our strength."

"Right. Yes." That's what I thought he meant. "I'm sure I won't stay up long. Catherine seemed disappointed, though," I add, because I like torture, apparently. "So were the other women." I force a chuckle.

He scratches the back of his head, then turns on the engine. "Yeah. They're not very subtle. But I don't think I'm leading them on. Am I? If so, it's not intentional."

I shake my head. "No, no. I didn't see any of that today."

"Okay, good. Because I'm really not interested." His gaze is currently burning through my skull, and I'm suddenly realizing just now how close we are in his car. It seemed so natural at first, but the way he's looking at me makes me keenly aware that we're both leaning toward each other.

"Why?" I breathe. "They seem like nice people, and they're good looking."

"Trust me, it's just the chef effect," he says with a long sigh. "The moment they realize this job takes most of my time, and I can't take care of them the way I should, they'd ask for the check and move on."

"Not all women are like that," I say, my mouth now so dry, the words scratch my throat.

His gaze drops to my lips, and I can feel the car heating up around us. Then, his eyes meet mine, full of hope and something I might describe as fear. "Maybe."

I swallow. "Some girls can understand, I'm sure."

He leans toward me, and a raging battle erupts in my brain. Should I let him kiss me, or run for the hills? He's getting closer, and I don't know which side I'm on. This was not part of the plan, and it'll make things so much more complicated. I don't live here. I don't *want* to live here, even if I do like Paris better now. But my heart won't survive another breakup. Not this soon. He's just inches away now, and I'm running out of time. Screw this. I can't overthink it. Only a few days with Olivier, and it feels like forever. Ever since last night's party, I've been dreaming of him kissing me again. I'm doing this. I want it.

I lean forward a few more inches, and a loud tune blasts through the car. We both jump in surprise, bumping our foreheads in the process.

"Gosh, sorry," he says, loud enough to carry over the sound as his hand reaches into his pocket. "Are you okay?"

Finding his phone, he presses a finger on the screen without detaching his eyes from mine.

"Yes. I'm fine," I say with a nod.

We're still looking at each other, not daring to move, when the phone blasts again. I tear my eyes from his and glance at his phone. Following my lead, he picks up without even looking.

And just like that, someone else made the choice for me.

Chapter 19

Olivier

I thought I hated Jean-Pierre, but now my feelings have boiled beyond hatred. He just *had* to ruin everything yesterday when he kept calling me like a maniac. I was *this* close to kissing Hazel, for real this time, and that's the moment he chose to ring me up about a freaking champagne tasting next week. Was it really that important to ask if I could go on a Friday night at eight? Couldn't it have waited until this morning?

After the call, the moment had passed, and Hazel went to bed as soon as we got home. I guess not all hope is lost, because I'm pretty sure she was about to kiss me back, but I don't know when I'll get my shot again.

We're now setting up everything for the event, and I can't help but admire the festival decór. The school event committee members really outdid themselves. The entire main street, which runs from the school to the church, has put on its fall colors. Arrangements of pumpkins and various squashes, mixed with hay bales and planters of autumn blooms, line the street between festival stands, and the trees with their sunset shades need no artifice to stand out.

Our stall is situated right next to the school's kitchen entrance so we can easily transport goods once they're cooked. We do have small ovens in the booth, and chafing dishes in the stalls, but the bulk of the food is reheated in the kitchen to keep things moving faster. Our stall is probably the longest too, easily fitting the eight of us. We narrowed our menu down to three savory and three sweet dishes, which means one person is in charge of serving each while Hazel and I are supervising and taking care of the behind-the-scenes action. Luckily, this arrangement also allows me to spend more time with her.

Since she doesn't speak French well, I don't want to leave her out on her own, especially since my family hasn't arrived yet. The festival just started a few minutes ago, and the first visitors are meandering down the street.

"Thank you again," I say to Hazel as we're pouring the *potimarron* and *cêpes velouté* in a thermos. "For helping with all this. It means a lot to me."

"Of course," she says, her eyes crinkling at the corners as she smiles. She looks absolutely stunning today—granted, she has every day since I met her—but this dark-green velvet skirt and the thin brown sweater she's wearing over it complement her figure and match her eyes perfectly. "It's my pleasure," she continues. "I had fun."

"Me too. It's been a while since cooking has been this enjoyable for me, so really, I mean it when I say thank you."

Our eyes plunge into each other again, and just when I'm wondering if I should just go for it, right here and now, I hear heels clacking on the tile floor followed by Catherine's voice.

"*On a besoin de velouté s'il vous plait*," she says.

She needs more velouté? Already? Though I'm surprised, I'm glad they're selling like hot cakes. Glancing at Catherine, I give her a slight nod and return to the cooker.

Of course this won't be the right time to kiss Hazel. Today is going to be mayhem, and it's just getting started.

The lunch rush has finally receded, and we've run out of most of the dishes we've prepared. Only a few *crêpes à la crème de marrons et aux poires* are left, as well as the pumpkin-spiced caramel apples.

Hazel is perched on the edge of a brick wall, drinking a bottle of water.

"Water?" I say with a severe frown. "We're at a fall festival. That's unacceptable."

She laughs. "What do you suggest?"

"Perhaps we can walk down the street? I'm sure we can do better than plain water."

With a grin, she nods and screws the lid on the bottle. "Sure."

Before we get going, I steal two caramel apples from our stand and hand her one. "We deserve it." I wink.

As we walk away, I feel a dozen eyes following our trail. It's only once we're out of ear's reach that Hazel releases a long swoosh of air.

"Glad it's over, huh?" I ask, bumping my shoulder with hers.

"Yeah, I'm grateful for a break." She giggles, closing her eyes. "These women do not like me."

I tilt my head to the side. "Oh, come on. You're very likable."

She gives me a pointed look. "Anyone who holds the title of 'Olivier's girlfriend' would be despised by those women. Even Mother Teresa."

With an embarrassed chuckle, I scratch my forehead. "Yeah, sorry. This gig was clearly more than you bargained for."

"Don't be. I asked to come, remember? I brought this upon myself," she says with a glint in her eye. "I guess it's a good thing I'm not living here."

Her words hit me like a filet knife in the chest. How can she say that when everything I've done these past few days was to make her *want* to live here? I'm clearly doing something wrong, or maybe it was just the PTA women who discouraged her.

"So, you're not going to take the job, then," I say. My tone is dry and firm. "You've decided."

She sighs, taking in the festive street filled with smiling guests. "That's what I'm leaning toward. Even if I do see why you love Paris now," she says, glancing at me with a smile. "But I don't know. It still feels so foreign, I'm nowhere near fluent, and I don't have anyone here."

"You have me."

She rolls her eyes, biting into her apple. "You know what I mean. Plus, we're not going to keep up this charade much longer. If we do, your mom will end up marrying us," she jokes with a laugh. I join in, but the thought scares me more than it amuses me. Or is it the fact that it doesn't amuse me at all, but *tempts* me that's scary?

"Yeah. You're probably right. But we could stay friends. People can maintain a friendship after they break up."

Her eyebrows shoot up. "Really? Is that a French thing? Because it rarely works on the other side of the Atlantic."

I wince.

"That's what I thought," she says, taking another bite of her apple.

"But there's always an exception to the rule, right?" I realize my tone sounds way too hopeful.

"Maybe."

We've now stopped in the middle of the way to gaze into each other's eyes. It's one of those moments when everyone is walking past you, but they seem transparent, like you're not really in the same place as them. My eyes linger on her face. I can't believe how lucky I am to be here, in this moment with this amazing girl. This time, I'm not letting anyone interrupt us.

Leaning forward, I caress her cheek with my free hand, and she shivers at the touch. Her hand runs along my forearm, sending tingles through my body. Closing my eyes, I press my lips against hers. They're as soft as I remember, but slightly sticky from the caramel. The sweetness tastes even better on her.

"*Ah, te voila,* Olivier." Mom's voice pulls me out of the moment.

Opening my eyes, I see her standing a few feet from us, holding the hands of both granddaughters.

I break away, and Hazel turns around to see my mother. At the same time, my nieces notice me and scramble toward us to give me a hug. I can't help but notice the blush on Hazel's cheeks deepening. Is that why she let me kiss her? Because she saw my family? Or maybe she assumes that's why I did it.

I don't have time to think it over, because the girls immediately steal us away to show us their favorite stalls and play some games with them. We play pop-a-pumpkin and ring toss. We're halfway through a game of Jack O'Lantern bean bag toss, enjoying every moment, when Mom and I step back from the line.

It's Hazel and Camille's turn, so we give them space.

"You seem happy with Hazel," Mom says, rubbing my back.

"Oui," I say, swallowing hard. Because it's the truth. I am happy with Hazel. And I haven't been this happy for a long time. *"Où est papa?"* I ask, hoping to change the subject. I don't really need to know where my dad is. He's probably at home mowing the lawn or whatever other activity he decided to do today to keep himself busy.

"Hazel is a beautiful girl and really nice. I like her a lot," she continues, not wanting to let this go. No need to remind me how amazing she is.

"And she loves your cooking," she adds.

"Oui." Well, that wasn't the case at the beginning, but I'm pretty sure all of that has changed now.

"I think that was the issue with the other girls," Mom continues. "They didn't fully appreciate you because they didn't take pleasure in eating your meals. They didn't understand you. Cooking is in your DNA."

"*Oui,* you might be right."

"Ah, it's my turn," she blurts, scurrying up to the throwing line.

As I watch Hazel walk toward me holding Camille's hand, I wonder if my mom could be right. It's true, cooking is a big part of me, and my exes never really cared about it. Sure, they ate my cooking, but they didn't appreciate it as much as Hazel does. Her passion for food matches mine, and that's why we match each other so perfectly.

Chapter 20

Hazel

Playing beanbag toss with Juliette and Camille brought me back to when Ivy and I were young. Mom used to take us to the school fair, and we'd begged her to let us stay just five more minutes. Somehow, we always ended up going home at closing time. Those were some of my favorite memories with her.

The twins both give me a big hug, and I pat their hair, chuckling.

"They like you," Agathe says with a warm smile.

"They're adorable." We stand side by side as we watch the girls skip over to their grandma. "But I don't know why they like me. I can't line up more than three words in French." I sigh, shaking my head. "I'm such a failure."

"Ah, don't beat yourself up. French is hard to learn, but I'm sure you'll pick up on it quickly." She nods to a nearby stall. "Want a drink?"

I nod and follow her. "Yeah. I think I'll get better, eventually."

"How are things going with Olivier? You guys look good together."

A blush warms my cheeks at her comment. I try to hide it as we order some coffee drinks.

"*Merci*," I say to the woman handing me my pumpkin-spice latte. With drinks in hand, we start walking. I was hoping Agathe would have forgotten about her question, but she's looking at me expectantly.

"It's going great." I try to plaster on a look of confidence, though my heart is prickling in my chest. "We're having fun. I've never laughed so much with someone." Which is absolutely true. A smile forms on my lips as I think about our pun-packed cooking sessions.

"Olivier was always the funny one, so it's good to have him back. He wasn't the same after what happened with his ex. He became more closed off and lost his sense of humor. I'm glad to see that sparkle of mischief back in his eye."

I know what she means. That sparkle is one of the things I love about him. It's hard to picture him without it.

"Oh, really?" I ask absently, sipping my pumpkin-spice latte "He never talks about her." I didn't want to pry, but the jealousy building in my core decided otherwise.

"Well, it was bad, very bad. But it's not my story to tell. Maybe he'll tell you one day," she says with a smile. Even though I really want to know, I'm glad he has people in his life protecting him instead of talking about him behind his back. "Matt always teases him, saying that he'll be single forever, but Olivier never seemed bothered by it. And I thought he didn't care. But now, I can see very clearly what was missing. Before you came along, he'd been looking so . . . What's the word?" she says, looking up. "Extinguished, maybe? And now he's glowing again. Night and day."

My blush intensifies. Could I really be the reason behind Olivier's mood change? Sure, we're having fun, but we're not even dating for real. Besides, I only met him ten days ago. "Thanks," I peep.

"Anyway, I'll stop now, or you might run," she says with a laugh. "I'm sure you already feel overwhelmed by Joelle. But I just wanted to say thank you, really. For bringing him back. And again, thank you for today. You didn't have to lend a hand. It's very gracious of you."

"Of course," I say, clutching my drink tighter as I try to wrap my head around everything she just said. "I was happy to help."

"Merci encore," a guy says, shaking Olivier's hand as we're packing up. *"C'était délicieux."*

"Merci à vous," Olivier says, beaming.

People have been stopping at our stall practically every minute to tell Olivier how good the food was and to thank him. Clearly, the menu was a hit. A feeling of pure joy washes over me. Not because I participated, but for Olivier's sake. He needed a reminder of how good his cooking is. He might have chosen the dishes to be family-friendly, appealing to kids as well as adults, but they were in no way less demonstrative of his gastronomic talents.

He deserves all the praise he's gotten today—and more. He's a wonderful man, generous, creative, kind. If only he was looking for a relationship, things might be different. I had almost made up my mind to call Jeff and accept the promotion, see where this could go between Olivier and me. I figured that maybe after his job situation got sorted, he might start dating again. But then, he kissed me. Another spectacular kiss that validated everything I was feeling, that reinforced my theory that we have a vibe, a connection. *Until* I saw his mom from the corner of my eye. Of course that was why he kissed me. There was no *vibe*. My hormonal brain had made that up entirely.

Chasing the thoughts out of my head, I follow him to the car to put away the last of the boxes before sliding into the passenger seat.

"Did you have a good day?" he asks, backing out of the parking space.

"I did. I'm so glad I had the chance to take part."

Turning to me, he smiles, showcasing that darned dimple again. "I'm sorry if my mom was overbearing, as usual," he jokes while adjusting the rearview mirror.

"Actually, she didn't say anything," I say, shaking my head.

"Phew." He laughs softly. "I feel like I should apologize every time she talks to you, though. Just in case. I love her, but she can be a lot sometimes."

"Don't worry. I know how it is. My mom was just like yours, only the American version."

"Really?" he asks with an encouraging smile.

"Yup. The first time she fixed me up was in kindergarten. She started early," I say, unable to suppress a giggle. "And she never stopped. As annoying as it was sometimes, I know it came from a place of love, and it's the same with your mom. It's just their way of making sure we're happy."

"And that they get grandbabies," he adds with a smirk. "I'm sure of it. And it worked with Matt. Believe it or not, Agathe was actually Mom's physiotherapist."

"Oh . . . I see. So, things might work out after all," I tease. "You should give it a try. Your mom might just have matchmaking super-powers."

He stops at a red light, then glances at me with a grimace. "Yeah, I'm not so sure about that."

I laugh, and we lock eyes for a minute. I can't seem to tear my gaze from his. There's a magnetic pull in the deep chocolate shade of his irises.

"You have the most unusual eyes, you know that?" he murmurs, and I shift in my seat.

A horn blares behind us, and I jerk my head to face the light. Who knows how long it's been green?

He presses on the gas again, and I look out the window. Watching a couple stroll down the sidewalk hand in hand, I venture, "Can I ask you a personal question?"

He glances toward me, then back to the road. "Sure. I'm always asking about you. It's only fair."

"What happened with your ex?" I peer at him to gauge his reaction. He's still looking straight ahead, hands on the wheel. "I was talking with Agathe and—"

"Oh, I see." He casts me a quick glance. "*La curiosité est un villain défaut*," he says, and I want to throw myself at him. That usually happens when he says more than three words in a row in French. Sue me.

"What does that mean?"

"It's a saying. I don't know if it exists in English. 'Curiosity is a bad trait'?"

My eyebrows shoot up. "Oh, yes. Curiosity killed the cat."

"Really? Wow. You guys are a lot more intense than us," he says with a dramatic whistle.

"We're Americans. The kings of drama," I joke. "Why do you think we invented Hollywood?"

"True," he says with a soft chuckle.

A short silence falls between us, and I hate it. I shouldn't have pried. It's none of my business.

"You don't have to—"

"Agathe has a big mouth, but I know she means well." He shakes his head. "My ex used me," he mumbles, gripping the wheel harder. "She was an up-and-coming food influencer when I met her, and she followed me around for some content."

"Oh."

"I fell for her, and we started dating. Except I was the only one committed in the relationship. She had another boyfriend, and she was just dating me to get her business going. She lied to me, to my family, and she did it without any remorse. She even encouraged me to open my own restaurant, offered to be a partner and everything. Then, she just disappeared."

Curiosity might very well kill the cat. Or maybe it's just me. A lump is now lodged in my throat, blocking my trachea. I don't think oxygen is even reaching my brain anymore. My mind is blank, my face is warm, and I think I'm going to faint.

"You okay?" he asks. Then, his hand settles on mine over the central console.

"Yeah," I say, jerking my hand back like I've just been bitten. "I'm just sorry that happened to you."

He pauses for a beat, then places his hand back on the wheel. "Me too."

With each passing mile, I try to calm down my breathing, counting the trees dressed in their fall foliage as we whiz past.

Reality just caught up with me, and it hit me hard in the face. Even if I'm starting to feel something for Olivier, and even if he *could* eventually develop feelings for me too—that's a huge *if*—he would never get over the fact that I lied to him. Not when it hits so close to home.

When I step out of the bathroom after my morning shower, I nearly bump into Olivier in the hallway.

"Hey," he says. "Sorry. Just ran out to the bakery to get some bread. Thought we could do a processed food breakfast again." He winks, showing off the long baguette in his hand.

My breath catches in my lungs. I don't know if it's the way his navy striped sweater hugs his muscles perfectly, or because of the baguette he's carrying, but Olivier's swoon level just demolished all previous records. The baguette. That has to be it. And that sweater. Stupid clichés.

"Is that okay? Did you want to eat something else? 'Cause I can—"

"No, no," I say with a smile. "I just got hit in the face with a cliché for a second, and I lost my words."

He laughs hard, twirling the stiff bread. "What? The baguette?"

"Yep," I say, biting my lip. "You're only missing the beret, and then the look will be complete."

He peers down at his chest. "Oh, right. Well, as I said, we don't really wear berets."

I heave an exaggerated sigh. "I know."

"Well, are you hungry?"

"Yes!" I say louder than intended. "I mean, you know me." I go for a more casual tone, but I'm not sure it's working.

After he makes a pot of coffee, we spread Nutella on our slices of bread before dipping them into the hot beverage. My new favorite thing.

"Mmm," I say. "It's so simple. But *berry* good."

I keep my head down but raise my eyes to peek at him. He's halfway through his bite. Swallowing, he wipes his mouth with his napkin. And just when I think my pun fell flat, and he didn't get it, he says, "I know. I like it a *latte*."

We both explode with laughter like a pair of teenagers. Or should I say, *a pear*?

Catching my breath, I hear the buzz of a notification on my phone and check it out.

French strike finally over after an agreement was reached this... The rest of the text doesn't fit in the email previewer.

"The strike is over?" I mumble, more to myself than Olivier, but he snaps his head toward me.

"What? Already?"

"Apparently." I click on the notification to read the full article, my heart stuttering with every word. Apparently, the strikers and the government have found a suitable compromise, and life will start to return to normal from today onward. I guess this is it, then. My heart twists painfully at the thought of leaving Paris. Leaving Olivier. But it's for the best. I'm falling for him, and if I stay, I'll only end up getting hurt. Again. Plus, I couldn't bear seeing the disappointment in his eyes if he found out who I am. It's not too messy—yet. The situation is still salvageable. Once I get back to the US, I'll forget him eventually and move on. I think . . . Probably.

"I'll look online to see if I can find a flight," I say, taking a sip of my coffee.

"Yeah. I'm happy for you. You're finally going home."

"Right." Our eyes meet, and I suddenly want to throw my phone away and jump into his arms. I wish I could tell him everything, declare my love for him and beg him to forgive me.

"I wanted to ask you something," he says, interrupting my thoughts. "But it might be bad timing."

I swallow hard. "Shoot."

"My boss asked me to go to a champagne tasting at a *château* near Epernay. It's about two hours away, in the Champagne region. I was wondering if you might want to go. But now you're getting ready to go home, so . . ."

"I'd love to. I mean, you know me. I'm not the type of girl to refuse a champagne tasting in a *château*," I joke, though it's true. I'm really not. Though I'm not sure there *is* a type of girl who would refuse that.

His eyes sparkle. "Oh, yeah? Okay. Great. It's only for two days, so we'll leave tomorrow afternoon and come back the next day."

"Perfect. In that case, I'll see if I can find a flight after that. One last French adventure before I go back."

He cocks his head to the side. "Yes. So *egg-citing*."

"Thank you very *matcha*," I say with a goofy smile, "for asking me to go with you."

"Of course." He winks. "Any-*thyme*."

Chapter 21

Olivier

The French are known for being revolutionary and everything, but let me tell you a secret. Give them a one-hundred-euro check, and they'll leave the pickets to bask in the comfort of their home. The revolutionary era is over.

As annoying as the strikes are, couldn't they have kept it up a little longer this time? Now, Hazel is looking at flights back to the US, and I'm running out of time.

I grip the wheel tighter during my commute to work. At least she's coming with me to Champagne tomorrow, so that's something to look forward to. A trip to a *château* and some bubbles might be just what she needs to realize that she likes me too. At least, that's what I'm hoping.

And with the number of tourists who'll be trying to get out of Paris right now, finding a flight won't be easy. Still, I've only got a few days, tops.

I have to step up my game, make her see how good we could be together, because I know there is a spark. I can feel it. With the way her last relationship ended, I understand her reluctance to step into something new, especially in a foreign city that has been, for the most part, a disappointment to her.

Then, a light bulb flickers on in my brain. I check the time on the car's display. I might be a few minutes late for work, but this is worth a try. At the next light, I take a right and drive for a few minutes until I reach a souvenir store with berets showcased in the front window. Did I already mention how desperate I am to make Hazel fall for me?

Once I finish my shopping, I head to work and only arrive five minutes late. But I'm the chef, so as long as I don't run into Jean-Pierre, it doesn't really matter.

My team is already hard at work when I enter the kitchen, and Jean-Pierre is nowhere to be found, thankfully. We go ahead with the usual preparations, but doing so immediately sends me back to that negative headspace and the familiar frustration that eats me from the inside.

Cooking these past few days was amazing. Fall has always been my favorite season. The fresh harvest and cozy vibes have my creativity flowing—with ideas I can't use. If I open my own restaurant, I'll be able to cook whatever I want. Change the menu every day, if I want to, shifting my offerings based on what I find at the market. I know some incredible farmers, and I love working with their produce, highlighting them. That's the real dream. Being inspired by nature and creating dishes that speak to me. Dishes I'm proud of. To treat people to new food combinations and see the twinkle in their eyes as they enjoy their meal with their loved ones. That's why I became a chef. Working in a palace and being a decorated professional was my dad's dream. Not mine.

I never realized, until now, how far my cuisine is from my dad's. That's why I hate this job so much. I'm not aligned with the food I'm making. He likes the posh, nothing-out-of-place vibe. Almost clinical. Meanwhile, I have more of a free-spirited cooking style. I like to see where my imagination takes me, roll with my ideas even if they're not always perfect. I like cozy comfort food with unexpected twists. Growing up, it always seemed obvious that I had to fill my father's shoes. So much so that I never even took a minute to ask myself if that was what I really wanted. But I think I inherited as much from my mom as I did from my dad when it comes to cooking. Elevating the simple tastes is one of my favorite things.

Images stream through my head like a movie, and in every one of them, Hazel is my co-star. She wears a glowing smile on her face as we live our dream together. My heart clenches at the thought. This is my dream, but is it hers? Reminders of my ex, and how I almost tasted my dream before she abandoned me, replace the beautiful picture in my brain. I can't let that happen again. This time, I won't back down. And hopefully, Hazel will be right there with me.

Hazel

When I wake up the next day, Olivier isn't here, so I hop in the shower and start packing some clothes for our trip. Hearing the lock click open, I wander out of my room to see if he wants help with breakfast. I'm kind of starving, but even if I'm comfortable here, I'd never touch anything in his kitchen without his consent. Not unless he was away and I was fending for myself.

When I step into the corridor, I turn around and gasp at the sight before me. Olivier. In a blue-and-white sweater. Holding a baguette. And wearing a freaking red beret.

Ooh, la la!

My arms fall to my sides, and my mouth hangs open in awe. Now I know why it's a cliché, and why it works. Olivier is sporting a cocky grin, clearly satisfied with the little prank he just pulled on me.

"*Bonjour*," he croons.

I open my mouth, then close it. There are no words. Nothing to express how incredibly sexy and gorgeous this man is right now, or how impossibly unfair this is.

"I thought you'd like it," he says, frowning as he steps toward me.

"It's—yeah, I like it," I stammer, nodding. "Very French. Well, from an American point of view, at least."

He chuckles. "I saw it in a souvenir shop on my way to work yesterday. Since you're leaving soon, I thought I'd give you at least one cliché," he says before dropping the baguette on the entryway table and taking out his phone from his pocket. As if I wasn't two seconds away from melting on the floor already, *La Vie en Rose* starts playing, and he extends his hand.

I know he's goofing around, but the tingling in my body is very much real as we start swaying to the music.

He sings along badly—on purpose—making a show of the situation. We bump into the entryway table and almost break his lamp, so we dance our way to the living room to enjoy more space. He's even a good dancer. Way better than me. I'm just a puppet, going along for the ride and hoping to survive it.

A loud gasp escapes me as Olivier dips me low when we reach the end of the song. This has never happened to me before. I mean, you need some strong muscles to dip me this low. Darn this man. Just when I was getting my heartbeat under control, he had to go and make this moment excruciating again. Our eyes lock, and I don't know how long I can hold on until I kiss this amazing guy. He's everything I hoped to find in a partner, and that's the exact reason why kissing him would be a disaster. The music ends, but he's not moving. His gaze intensifies, and I look away, clearing my throat.

"The baguette is real, right? I'm kind of starving."

He lifts me back up and takes a step back. "Right. No. Yes, it's real." He scratches his head. "Let's have some breakfast."

Oof. That was a close call.

Once we're done eating, we each prepare an overnight bag for our trip to Champagne. I have to admit, I'm really looking forward to it. Even if it does mean I'll be tortured for the next day and a half. Sometimes, I worry about my sanity. Let's just hope he's not taking his beret.

I'm zipping up my bag when my phone rings, and my stomach drops. I managed to get Jeff off my back about the pending reviews after telling him I choked during a meal and had to be rushed to the hospital. Yes, I'll admit I did exaggerate things a little, but I had no choice. And yes, I do realize how deep of a hole I've dug myself. Covering a lie with another one is never a good idea, and you always get caught. Maybe I'm about to.

I sigh in relief when I see Ivy's face on the screen. I throw myself on the bed, my forehead wrinkling. Why is she calling so late?

"Ivy," I say, picking up. "What's wrong? Are you okay?"

"I'm engaged!" she yells, showing off her hand on the tiny screen. But it's moving so much, I can't see anything. Though the background is dark, I'm pretty sure she's on a beach.

"Wow."

"Yes!" She jumps up and down. "It happened about two hours ago. We had a romantic dinner on the beach, then we danced. Oh my gosh, Hazel, it was perfect."

Even through the darkness, I can see the sparkle in her eyes, and my heart leaps for joy for my sister. Or is it a clenching feeling of hurt?

"That's fantastic, Ivy. So, he's the one, then?" I ask, flipping onto my back. "He makes you happy?"

She bursts into loud giggles. "Of course. We've been together for two years. If he didn't, I wouldn't be with him anymore."

"Okay. Sorry, I'm the big sister. I had to ask." To tell the truth, I never really liked him, but hey, I'm not the one marrying him. If Ivy's happy, so am I.

"It's everything I've ever dreamed of. And we've already decided on a winter honeymoon. I wanted a snowy wedding, but we settled for a honeymoon in the mountains. In a way, it's even better."

"You have a date for the wedding already?" I ask, trying to hide the surprise in my tone.

"Yes! Christmas Eve next year. That way, we can enjoy the December Floridian weather for the wedding before cozying up in the mountains afterwards. You know how much I want to see snow, and how Dan hates it. So, we made a compromise."

"That sounds perfect." I force a big smile. "I'm happy for you."

"Thanks! Anyway, enough about me. What's going on with you and the Frenchie?" she asks, arching her eyebrows.

I pick at a loose thread of fabric on the bed cover. "Nothing."

She snorts loudly. "Oh, come on. You blush every time I bring him up, and half of your texts are about him."

"Shh." I glance behind me. The last thing I need is for Olivier to hear I have a crush on him.

"Then tell me."

"Fine," I whisper. "He's gorgeous, and I'm completely in the *merde*, Ivy. He's probably the nicest, funniest, most generous guy I've ever met. But he doesn't want a relationship, and we live on different continents. So there's that."

"Oh, wow. It's more than just a little crush, then? You're falling for this guy."

"Thanks for the reminder. And I challenge anyone to spend time with Olivier and *not* fall for him. I mean, the guy showed up with a beret and a baguette this morning. How am I supposed to resist that? And now, I'm going on an overnight trip with him to a château in Champagne."

"Oh my stars!" She clasps her hand over her mouth. "Really? Now I'm jealous. You should definitely go for it. Even if it all ends in a few days."

I resist the urge to sigh. The thing is, I'm not sure I'd be able to leave if anything were to happen with him. I shake the thought away. It doesn't matter, because it takes two to tango. "It won't happen, Ivy. He just got out of a bad relationship, and he's not looking for anything. Not even a fling." As if I'd be satisfied just having a fling with him.

"Well, you were in the same boat, if I recall. 'Not my season of love,' blah blah blah," she says in a very poor imitation of me. "Maybe he changed his mind too, you know?"

The idea makes my heart flutter. But then, it sinks again. Even if he did, I'd bring him right back to that place when he learned about my job and the fact that I lied to him.

"Anyway, all I'm saying is that you should go for it, Hazel. You'll regret not taking the chance. I'm newly engaged and over the moon in love, so the fact that a teeny tiny part of me is jealous right now is telling. But I thought French men didn't wear berets?" she asks, frowning in confusion.

"They don't."

Her eyebrows scrunch together. "But he does?"

"No."

"So, he bought a beret for *you*."

I swallow hard, because that's exactly what happened, and the gesture was incredibly sweet.

"Um, Hazel. If a Frenchman buys a beret for your sake, you say *merci* and jump into his arms," she scolds. "Where are your manners?"

That makes me laugh out loud. I miss Ivy so much. "Don't you have a fiancé to get to? Did he leave you on the beach or something?"

She giggles, looking behind her. "No. He's getting champagne from the hotel lobby. We're going to sleep on the beach tonight. It's no château, but it will do."

I chuckle. "Well, have fun, you lovebirds."

"*Merci*. You too."

I end the call, but the conversation lingers in my head. Should I give in to one last hurrah with Olivier? Explore these feelings, get a taste, even if I know it won't last? My body heats at the thought, and I fan myself. No. Nothing good would come of it. It's not me. I don't do casual. And anyway, why am I conjuring up stupid scenarios in my head when he probably doesn't even want that with me? My mind is just jumbled with all the emotions being thrown at me—and that stupid beret. This is just a champagne-tasting trip between friends, and that's how we'll play it.

I straighten myself, grab my bag, and step out of the room. Olivier is in the hallway, putting his coat on.

He holds back a beaming smile. "All *bready* to go?"

The corner of my mouth twitches into a grin. "Yup. It's going to be a *grape* day."

Energized by the sound of our laughter, we pile out of the house.

Champagne, here we come.

Chapter 22

Hazel

The drive to Champagne is pleasant, and I embrace every minute of it because I know that once we arrive, and Olivier starts speaking French again, my body is going to endure all sorts of fluttering and ridiculous temperatures. Resisting his charm during this trip is going to be particularly excruciating. I just hope he really did leave his beret at home.

During the car ride, we listen to popular French music on the radio, and I discover a couple of artists I really like—Christophe Maé and Vianney. As the music plays gently, we talk about our childhoods. I just finished telling him about losing my mom a few years back and growing up without a father.

"I'm sorry," he says with a comforting smile. "I can't imagine losing my mom, but I grew up with an absentee father, so I know how painful that is."

"But he was working. That's different. He was providing for you and your family. Mine just didn't want anything to do with us."

"It felt like that for us too. Even Matt says it. Our dad was more interested in his work than spending time with us. You've seen him. Always on his own, trying to find something to occupy his time. Anything to avoid being with us because he doesn't know how. Doesn't know us."

"Sorry. That's tough. You still have a shot of changing things, though. You should talk to him about it."

He sucks in a breath. "Well, once I tell him I'm quitting the palace and opening my own restaurant, he's probably going to disown me. So our relationship isn't going to change any time soon."

I snap my head toward him with a gasp. "You're opening your own restaurant?"

He gives me a sheepish smile. "I think so, yeah. I've been looking at a couple of places that have potential, and then I'll get a proposal ready for the banks."

A tingling sensation sweeps through my chest. "Oh my goodness, Olivier. That's wonderful! I'm so happy for you."

His smile widens, revealing that adorable dimple. "Thank you. And thanks for pushing me and reminding me what cooking is all about."

My eyebrows shoot up. "I did that?"

"Of course you did. Last week, we had so much fun cooking together. I'd forgotten about that joy, somehow, and I don't want to lose it ever again."

"I'm so glad I could help, and that you found your passion again. It's going to be fantastic. What kind of restaurant are you going for? What are you planning to serve?"

He shoots me a glance, his eyes sparkling. "I'm leaning more towards comfort food. Well, elevated comfort food. I want to take simple food items and dishes and give them a unique twist. I want to surprise people but still be accessible, you know? I don't want to overcomplicate things. I don't know. Maybe it's dumb, and I should stick to high gastronomy."

"No," I blurt out louder than intended as I almost jump in my seat. "What you're describing is perfect. It's exactly what I picture when I think about you opening your restaurant. Elevating simple dishes. Just like you did this past week."

His eyes land on me again. "Yes. Exactly."

"It's going to be incredible, Olivier. I just know it." My heart warms, but then breaks when I remember that I won't be on this journey with him. "Let me know when you open. I'll definitely fly over and check it out."

He smiles, but it feels forced. "Oh yes, of course." Then, he focuses back on the road, his hands gripping the wheel tight.

Château Lacombe is gorgeous. The imposing century-old building made of white stone with creeping ivy on the corners stands on a sprawling property, the closest neighbors being miles away. It's the perfect estate for a romantic escapade. Work. *Work* escapade.

The owner, Luc—a fifty-something guy with kind eyes and a large beard—welcomes us with open arms, giving us a tour of the place and showing us our *separate* rooms. Mine is a cute white-and-pink suite featuring a queen-sized bed, a beautiful carved dresser, and a matching dressing table. Very castle-like.

After we settle in, he suggests we go straight for a champagne tasting along with some lunch.

"So," Luc says once we're in the cellar. It's a narrow, windowless room stocked with wooden barrels. The smell of damp wood that mingles with aging wine overwhelms my senses, and I'm already getting dizzy. "We are a very small *domaine* producing only forty thousand bottles per year."

"That's small?" I ask. It feels like a big number.

"Oh *oui*," Luc says. "Moet and Chandon, for example, produce twenty-six million bottles a year. Veuve Clicquot, twenty-two million. So yes, we are very tiny next to them."

I blink a few times. "Oh, wow. Okay."

"We harvest all of our grapes ourselves, which is naturally impossible for the bigger houses, who outsource the production to independent winemakers. We have five acres of vines right here around the *château,* which we'll go see afterwards. I'm the third generation of winemakers in my family after my father and grandfather. We aim to produce a champagne of exceptional quality, and all of our exports are certified high environmental value, the highest level of environmental certification here in France. We also press the grapes in house. Let me go grab a few bottles, and we can start the tasting."

"I'm excited," I tell Olivier once Luc is gone. "Sounds promising. I've only ever tasted brand names when it comes to champagne."

"I always stay away from brand names. They can't match the quality of small houses. Except maybe with their highly prestigious bottles, like Dom Perignon for example, but the price tag isn't the same, and I've tasted far better champagne for a fraction of the price."

"Have you tried Luc's champagne yet?"

"No. As he mentioned, they're a very small producer, which makes them very exclusive. They only sell to people they know. My boss and sommelier have been trying to expand our wine list with smaller brands for a while, but most of them refuse because they don't have enough bottles to sell. That's why my boss asked me to make this trip when our sommelier got sick. It's a rare opportunity."

And once again, I find myself benefiting from Olivier's connections. No matter how many times it happens, it doesn't get easier. If anything, it only twists the knife further into the heart of the liar I am.

I force a smile and take a deep breath. These are my last days with him, and I should try to enjoy my time. Plus, it's not like I'm going to write a review on Luc's champagne.

Yes, I know I'm trying hard to convince myself I'm not a terrible person. And no, it's not working. Yet. But maybe after a few glasses . . .

Luc returns holding various bottles and glasses along with a tray of cheese. I like him more and more by the minute. He brings a cheese plate with bread for the three of us. "First, let's try our ambassador *cuvée*. It's an *extra brut* champagne—meaning between zero and six grams of added sugar per liter. Incredibly fresh with notes of yellow fruits, white flowers, and a saline finish."

He pours each of us a glass. *"Santé,"* they both say as I utter, "cheers."

Just as Luc said, this champagne is very crisp, and I'm surprised by this saline finish. I've never tasted that before, in a wine or a champagne.

"*Très bon,*" Olivier gushes. "*Parfait pour l'apéritif.* A great palate opener."

They dive into a conversation in French, and I try to focus on my food and drink. The second champagne is the same variety we just tasted but in *brut*, which, as Luc explains, means there's between six and twelve grams of added sugar per liter. The difference is striking. I can still taste those yellow fruit notes, but it's as if they're riper, and the saline taste has vanished, leaving a richer mouth feel.

Then, we move on to their *blanc de blanc*—which is made only of chardonnay—and their *blanc de noirs,* made only of their pinot noir grapes. That last one might be my favorite. It's a lot richer and more wine-like than the blanc de blanc, which is pretty dry.

"*Délicieux,*" Olivier says, licking his lips. Oh, the weird things it does to my body, sending prickles of pleasure all over and leaving me feverish. Olivier is really hot. Like, yeah, I knew he was hot. But not *this* hot. How have I managed to resist him all this time? If Luc wasn't here, I don't think I'd be able to hold off.

"Should we go for a walk in the vineyard, then?" Luc offers, startling me with the loud pitch of his voice. "We'll try our vintage champagne tonight over dinner. It'll be a more appropriate setting for it."

I glance at Olivier, who's standing up as if Luc's voice didn't just shatter the cellar, making my head pound. There's a slight frown wrinkling his forehead, and he mouths, "Are you okay?"

I nod, eating one last piece of cheese. I need some food in my system ASAP. And some fresh air.

The tour of the vineyard left me enchanted with its endless rows of vines interspersed with towering oak trees. Plus, the chilly weather was exactly what I needed to put my thoughts back in order after the tasting.

Thank goodness for Luc being here, or this whole experience would be way too romantic for my taste. Luc is passionate about what he does, and he's happy to explain everything about champagne and the fabrication process, which has left me enraptured. I love to learn new things, and it was the perfect distraction. From the manual harvesting of the grapes to the aging part, I'm surprised how complex the whole process is, and I found myself eager to know more. He also gives me a crash course on champagne in general, and I'm impressed by the number of varieties packed into such a small region. We drink more and more champagne throughout the tour, and by the time we're done, I can't even feel my feet anymore. Good thing, though, because they must be in bad shape after all the walking we did, not to mention my totally inappropriate flat shoes.

Luc's chef has prepared a dinner for us to pair with their most complex champagne, and Olivier is currently chatting with him while I freshen up in my room. At least, that's what I told them I was doing. In reality, I've just downed half a bottle of water and am now nearly passed out on my bed.

When I stand up, the room still spins a little. Maybe I just need some more food in my stomach. As I trudge down the stairs, Olivier appears at the bottom, looking as sexy as he's been all day with his cute olive sweater that clings to his muscles and complements his eyes perfectly.

His hair is tousled from walking against the wind, which leaves me wanting to rake my hands through it even more. Our eyes meet, and I can't break from his magnetic pull. The way he looks at me always makes me feel powerful. Dare I say, *wanted*?

I miss the last step and lose my balance, falling straight into the strong arms of Olivier, who was right there to catch me.

"Wow, are you okay?" he asks with a chuckle.

"I'm fine." I steady myself on his shoulders, and we stand there for a second, his hands burning on my waist. "I lost my balance. It might be the champagne," I say with a touch of humor. Either that, or Olivier's stare.

Yep, we have our winner.

"You have to eat and drink some water. Come." Of course *he* looks perfectly normal, like he hasn't drunk a drop of champagne. It must be a French thing. Their internal systems are practically made for wine tastings.

He takes me by the hand. The gesture feels so natural, I don't say a thing. The dinner table is beautifully decorated, and the scent wafting from the kitchen smells heavenly.

Dinner is sumptuous, and the champagnes Luc pours us are all exceptional, but the last one is definitely my favorite. It beats every wine I've ever tasted.

"There's so much depth and structure. I love it," I say, swirling it in my glass.

Luc beams at me. "*Merci*. Yes, this one is very complex."

"I agree," Olivier says. "It's round and sensual. Elegant." His eyes are trained on me as he speaks, and my entire body catches fire when I realize he's not only talking about the champagne.

I detach my gaze from his and try to focus on Luc, who's telling us about this specific blend.

"Excuse me. I'm going to offer my congratulations to the chef," Olivier says, finally pulling his eyes away from me.

After finishing his monologue about champagne and answering my questions, Luc decides to call it a night.

"Feel free to stay up for as long as you want. Please, finish the bottle. There's more in the wine cooler if you're interested," he says with a wink. "I'll go say goodnight to Olivier."

"*Merci beaucoup*, Luc. *Bonne nuit*."

Minutes later, Olivier steps back out from the kitchen, and the fact that the two of us are now alone here with a bottle of champagne makes me very aware of how dangerous this situation is. I know I should really go to bed. But at the same time, this is one of my last nights in France. With Olivier. And there's no way we can let the rest of that champagne go to waste.

"Another glass?" Olivier asks, arching an eyebrow as he sits back down next to me.

"*Wine* not?"

Chapter 23

Olivier

Laughing with Hazel will never get old. We're both drunk right now, but I'm proud of us for still managing to come up with new puns.

"You know," she says, giggling, "I've heard that champagne is good for your *pours*." Then, she sets off again, and I'm having trouble catching my breath.

"Well, then. Hit me, baby, one more *wine*."

Collapsing onto the table, she explodes into laughter, tears springing from her eyes. "Oh my goodness. Yay for Britney."

For a second, I forget everything else, because Hazel looks magnificent, blinding me with her beauty. Her hair is adorably messy, the sparkle in her eyes is competing with the bubbles trailing up the bottle, and her smile—her smile is captivating. A full-on tooth smile that almost hurts at the corners. I know because I'm sporting the same one.

Reaching for her face, I capture the tears falling down her cheek.

Her eyes fall to my lips.

"You're so beautiful," I whisper.

Giggling, she leans into my hand, and I cup her face. "You're not so bad looking yourself. Especially with that beret." She breaks into a fit of laughter again, and my smile widens.

"I got it just for you."

"I know." She bites her lip, her gaze drawn to mine. "Why?"

"Because you were dreaming of a Frenchman with a beret?" I say, hoping it doesn't sound as pathetic as it actually is. "I was just trying to make that dream come true."

"There's only one Frenchman I want," she says, jabbing my torso with her finger, "with or without a beret."

My heart leaps, and suddenly, I'm extremely heady. "Really?"

She nods, another giggle escaping her lips. "You're the *wine* that I want."

Is this really happening? I want to pinch myself just to make sure, but I don't have to. I see it in her eyes. In the way her chest rises and falls with every rapid breath. I feel it in the air thickening around us. "I am, huh?"

"Mm-hm." Her forehead presses against mine, and I trace a finger along her soft lips.

"Are you going to kiss me?" she asks, glancing up.

"Do you want me to?"

"Yes," she answers. "But I want a proper French kiss this time. With tongue and everything."

She doesn't have to ask me twice.

Our mouths collide, and I'm transported to another world. A world of hope and brighter futures. A world where Hazel lives in France with me, and all our dreams come true. A world where I can feel the softness of her lips and her heart beating against mine every single day. Where every inch of her is familiar and comforting. Where she and I are the happiest couple on the planet.

I never want this to end.

When I wake up the next day, I almost wonder if it was all a dream. Kissing Hazel, her telling me I'm the one she wants. But I know it was real, because even the best dreams can't make you feel what I felt last night. My heart burst into pieces, and my entire world became everything I'd ever hoped for.

But as the morning wears on, I'm getting more anxious by the second, because I wonder if it was just the champagne talking. Did she mean all those things she said? Maybe she doesn't even remember saying them.

When I get down to breakfast, she's already sitting at the table eating a crêpe—my girl—with Luc seated right in front of her.

"*Olivier, comment ça va? Bien dormi?*"

"*Bonjour. Oui, très bien.* A bit hungover, but it was a wonderful evening," I say, my gaze turning to Hazel. Her beautifully complex brown-green eyes are set on me, and I know the memory of last night is etched in her brain too. Hopefully, it's a good one.

"I'm glad you enjoyed it," he replies with a grin. "Breakfast?"

"Sure."

Hazel doesn't say much during breakfast, then she disappears while Luc and I talk business. He's interested in having his champagne on the Cezanne table, and we take a few minutes to set up a test dinner. I also come clean about my intent to leave the palace and start my own venture. To my utmost surprise, he says he'd be more than happy to discuss a collaboration with my new place as well.

Finally, the time comes to return to Paris, and I'm eager to get into the car with Hazel. We haven't really spoken much this morning, so I don't know how she feels about last night. We say goodbye to Luc before starting our journey back.

Silence hangs over us until we reach the highway. I've been meaning to say something, but I forget it every time I open my mouth.

A notification pings on her phone, and she pulls it out of her bag. "Oh, I'm finally off the waiting list," she says. "I've been put on a flight for tomorrow night."

That announcement almost sends me over the edge. "What?"

"Yeah." She glances at me, her big hazel eyes softening before she brings them back to her phone.

I try to focus on the road. "You can't go, Hazel. Please don't go." There, I said it. I didn't need some elaborate speech after all. Just what comes from the heart.

"Olivier . . ."

"Yesterday. It was—"

"I know." She breathes out a heavy sigh.

I cast her a tentative glance, but she's peering out the side window. "Then you know you can't leave."

The utter quiet that meets my words is killing me softly inside. Spotting a rest area, I decide to pull over. We need to have this conversation face to face.

When I park, we both get out of the car. The rest area is relatively empty, only a few cars pumping gas in the distance. We're now parked near an overflowing trash can. Not exactly your ideal romantic venue.

I take her hand in mine. "Please, Hazel. I know you feel it too. What we have—"

"I do," she says, and an unsure smile tugs at her lips. "But your job and the restaurant . . . You told me you wanted to focus on your career, and I don't want to derail your plans."

I caress her cheek. "There is no plan without you. You're the one who nudged me in the right direction. I wouldn't imagine pursuing my dream without you by my side."

Her brow wrinkles as she raises her head to meet my gaze. "You wouldn't?"

"I'll need a sous chef for my restaurant, won't I? And I have my eyes set on you."

She opens her mouth to speak, but I'm quicker. "I know you already have a job that you love. But maybe you could cut down your hours. You could do part-time university, part-time kitchen." I fully realize I'm rambling now, and I need to stop before she runs away.

She cocks her head to the side. "You've really thought this through."

I let out a small laugh and squeeze her hand. "How could I not? We're amazing together, in and out of the kitchen. I can't imagine not having you in my life. These past few days have—"

"Been incredible," she finishes, her face beaming, and I pull her close. Pressing my forehead against hers, I breathe her in. Never before have all my dreams been so close within reach.

We stay like that for a second before she shuffles a step back, shaking her head. "But this is crazy. I don't even know if I'm ready for a relationship, and I live thousands of miles away."

Taking a step forward, I pull her near me again and stare into those beautiful hazel eyes. "I know this is fast, but please let me take care of you. You deserve it. I want nothing more than to make you feel as amazing as you are. I'll wear that damn beret every day if I have to."

"Olivier, wait," she mutters, placing a hand on my torso. "It's—I need to—"

"Hazel," I cut in before kissing her soft lips. "We can figure it all out. Don't overthink this."

I slide my hand to her neck and kiss her again. Deeper this time as I strive to show her how much I need her to say yes. How much I want to make her happy. Make *us* happy.

She resists at first, but after a moment, she wraps her arms around my back, and I finally feel like I can breathe again.

When we arrive home, we do what we do best together—we cook. And kiss.

"Were you serious about me working in your restaurant?" she asks as we're digging into the blue cheese ravioli we just prepared.

I swallow my bite. "Of course I was."

She pins me with an incredulous stare. "Really? I mean, it'd be an honor—you know how much I love food—but I have no experience in a professional kitchen. There are far more talented people who deserve to work under a chef like you."

"A kitchen brigade is composed of more than two people," I say with a chuckle. "But I've seen you at work these past few days. You're excellent. You have great instincts, and you're a fast learner."

She wrings her hands and averts her eyes. "I don't know."

"Whose idea was it to add crushed nuts to the meal we're eating now?" I ask, arching an eyebrow.

She concedes a smile. "Okay, fine, this one time."

"Well, it's a start. You see the difference it makes in the dish. The nuts are a great addition. You did good."

Pausing, she nods. "*Salami* get this straight." She bursts into giggles, unable to finish her sentence, and I laugh along. Finally catching her breath, she continues, "You were basically evaluating me all this time without my knowledge?"

I take another bite. "Yup. And you passed with *frying* colors."

Her eyes sparkle as she erupts into a fit of laughter, a hand over her ribs. "You're *kiwing* me."

I cock my head to the side, throwing her a questioning look. "*Soda* think you can help me out?"

As her laughter subsides, she shakes her head. "It's hard to know if you're serious right now."

"Oh, but I'm very serious. I want to do this with you."

Her face relaxes, and she leans into me. "I'd be honored to help."

Grabbing her chin, I plant a soft kiss on her luscious lips, once again left in awe of how lucky I am that the universe put this girl in my path. "Well, *lettuce* celebrate, then!"

Chapter 24

Hazel

I'm sitting at the kitchen bar, crafting and recrafting my email to Jeff, not sure how I'm going to word it. He sent me here in the hopes that I'd move to Paris to work for him, and now I'm gearing up to tell him that I will indeed move here, but that I'm resigning?

There's no easy way to phrase this. Even Jeff's cheery mood is going to take a punch with this one. Of course, I'm not going to leave him high and dry. I can keep my position for a few months, even help him find a replacement who already lives here in Paris.

I've also stayed up most of the night debating whether to write my reviews about the second round of restaurants I visited. I know that sending those along would soften the blow. But in the end, I decided not to. I'll tell Jeff not to pay me for that portion of the trip. It would be unethical to write them. I didn't pay for the meals, and I've met all the chefs. They were all amazing and generous, even if some elements of their cuisine could be improved. Plus, now that I know the dramatic consequences a bad review can have, I don't want to keep writing them. I know they're meant to spur improvement, but a bit of research showed me that many Michelin star chefs end up in depression—or worse—when they lose stars. And while I'm not the one awarding them, it still feels like I'm part of the process, and I don't like it.

Ivy's face appears on my phone as it vibrates. We've been messaging since yesterday, and through most of the night, so she's officially caught up on my personal drama.

I put the conversation on speaker. "Hey, you're up early."

"About to go to sleep, actually," she says with a yawn. "Night shift at the hospital."

"Oh, right. How was it?"

"Slow night. So, good." She cracks her neck to each side. "Oh! Speaking of work, did you spill the beans to Olivier?"

I moan. "No, not yet."

Another thing that's been keeping me up all night. The sword of Damocles has been lowering dangerously these past few days. Ever since Jeff said the reviews would be published "soon." But the blade hasn't fallen yet.

I know I'm lucky. It's like the universe is offering me a chance to come clean before it's too late, but I can't. I was so close to telling him yesterday. But every time, I chickened out. I need to rehearse exactly how I'm going to reveal my big secret. I only have one chance at this, and I can't blow it.

"Hazel!" Ivy scolds. "You have to tell him. You said you'd do it this morning."

"I know. I know, but he was so amazing, and I really, *really* like him, Ivy. I think we have a serious shot. I don't want to mess it up."

"Where is he now?"

I blow out a heavy sigh. "At the market. I said I had to write my resignation email, so he went alone."

"Well," she scolds, her reproachful tone back on, "You have to come clean. The longer you wait, the worse it's going to be."

I twist my lips as my heart wrenches. "I know, but I want to resign first. That way, when I tell him, it'll already be a thing of the past, you know? And I want to choose my words carefully."

"That doesn't make much sense to me. Words won't change the truth. Tell him now and send the email later. What if he wants nothing to do with you once he finds out? You did say that was a possibility."

My throat constricts at the thought. "I know. But I'm hoping it won't go down like that. The things he said to me . . . I think he likes me as much as I like him."

"Well, either way. You have to tell him and fast."

I swallow hard. "I will."

As if on cue, just when I hang up, I hear the front door opening.

"Hey," Olivier greets as I join him at the door to help with the bags. "How's the email going?"

"Not great," I say, ignoring the lump of lead in my stomach.

"I can imagine. I'm not quite ready to have that conversation with Jean-Pierre either." He grimaces. "I'll wait until I find a location for the restaurant, though. That can take a while. I also have to talk to the banks and so on."

Bobbing my head, I help him with the groceries before sitting back at the bar, staring at the blank document I have open.

I've opened a blank document on my laptop, trying to write down what I would tell Olivier, but I've been rewriting the same two sentences for the past twenty minutes, and I hate everything. I thought it'd be easier to see the words and rearrange them before I confront him, but no matter how I put my confession, it's still awful.

Olivier, I have to tell you something. When we met, I said I was a historian, but that's not exactly true. While I do hold a deep love for history, and Paris is a great place to be for that—

Seriously? I press the Backspace key until the page is blank again. I need to be more direct.

Olivier, I lied to you. I am not a historian but a food critic. When we met, I was really evaluating your restaurant.

Maybe not that direct? Gosh, this is impossible. No matter how I lay this on him, he's going to hate me. I'm sure of it now.

"Hazel?" Olivier utters, his pitch rising. He stands up from the couch, phone in hand. His wide eyes meet mine, and shock is written all over his face. "You're a *food critic?*"

The last word gets stuck in his throat, as if it doesn't want to come out. And I can't blame him for not wanting to say it out loud. Those simple words have terrible consequences.

Blood drains from my face as my brain rushes to put words together to form a coherent sentence, but nothing comes out.

"Dull," he reads, eyes glued to his phone. "A cuisine that clearly lacks passion and creativity. High hopes for the son of a gastronomy legend who didn't deliver on the promi–"

His eyes close, and he drops his phone on the couch.

I scurry toward him, reaching forward to take his hand, but he takes a step back, his face reddening as he pulsates with anger. His usual warm and sparkling eyes become two dark holes as he bears an expression that's a mix of shock and fury.

"*C'est pas possible,*" he mumbles, shaking his head slightly. "*Ça recommence. Tu m'as menti...*"

"Olivier, you're speaking French," I say, even though I'm pretty sure I know what he's saying. That I'm a big fat liar.

"You lied to me. You're not a historian. You're... You're a food critic?" he asks, staggering another step back, like he's just been shot in the stomach. "HC from *Miami Taste*. That can only be you. Those words, you said them to me that night. I remember."

I venture another tentative step toward him. "Olivier, I can explain. I'm so sorry. I wanted to tell you, but I couldn't. When we met, I—"

Closing his eyes again, he huffs out a forceful breath. "Please, just go," he says, slumping onto the couch and staring into space.

"What? No." I sit down next to him, placing a hand on his knee. He grabs my hand and removes it at once, and the chill of his touch sends shivers down my spine. "I wrote that review before I knew you. I'm sorry. Please, we can figure this out."

"No, Hazel. We can't." He turns to me, and then I see it—the mix of disappointment, hurt, and hatred brewing in his eyes. They start to redden, glassing over, and now I'm the one who's just been shot. Or maybe I've been stabbed, because I can almost feel my insides writhing deep in my gut. "You messed everything up. I don't want you here anymore. Please, just go."

"Olivier," I plead. "We have to talk about this."

He springs up from the couch. "I can't do this, Hazel," he shouts, a sour expression marring his face. "We had fun, we fooled around, and now it's over. I don't have time for this."

My heart sinks. "'Fooled around'? Is that what you think we were doing? We were making plans for the future together."

"Don't twist this around. Just go. Please." His tone is calm yet firm, and it's icing my body out.

"Olivier, please. I *had* to lie when I was reviewing your restaurant. Then, I just got caught up in it. I didn't know how to tell you. It's—"

"Get out, Hazel," he booms, his eyes bloodshot.

My lips quiver, and I do my best to hold the tears in. "Fine. But for the record, I thought what we had was real."

His head snaps toward me. "*Real* requires honesty, Hazel. And you lied to me from day one."

A tear escapes his eye, sliding down his cheek, and it's too much for me to handle. My own tears blur my vision as I grab my computer and rush to my room.

I hastily pack my stuff up. When I return to the living room, he's not on the couch anymore. It's probably better that way. One last look at him, injured by my actions, and my heart might shatter into a thousand pieces.

Olivier

I can't believe it happened again. What's wrong with me? Is there a sign that says 'lie to me' or 'take advantage of me' hanging on my forehead or something?

I chuck the grocery bag to the other side of the room.

I really thought things were different this time. Never in a million years would I have thought we'd end up this way. Hazel was mending her heart just as much as I was—or so I thought—and that made me vulnerable. Or was she lying about that too? How can I know what's even true at this point?

All the moments we spent together play before my eyes. With every smile, every laugh, every kiss that we shared, it hurts just a little more. Now, everything makes sense. Her knowledge about high gastronomy, her passion for food, why she wanted to try out restaurants while she was stuck here, why we even met in the first place. How did I not see any of it?

She was eating alone that night. That should have tipped me off. Except that clue in itself doesn't really mean anything. These days, a lot of people dine alone. It's not even remotely suspicious anymore.

Plus, we know for a fact that critics—at least Michelin guide critics—come in groups or with their loved ones to stay incognito, because dining alone is way too obvious. Yet here we are.

And the words she used in her review. So cold, so harsh. I know I hadn't prepared my best meal that night, but did I really deserve those scathing descriptions? Boring, dull, lacking in creativity and passion. Those words break careers. And in this case, they also crush hearts. And I don't have to think twice to decide which one hurts most.

Chapter 25

Olivier

The doorbell rings, and my heart leaps. I glance at the window, but it's dark outside. And the glass is on the side of the house anyway. What if it's Hazel? What if she came back? Wait. Do I even want her to come back? I pace around the room, debating whether to answer. Just like how I've been hesitating to call her for the past two days. I actually did cave and call her once, but I ended the call before it went through. Then, I turned my phone off to prevent any more slip-ups. Because as much as I miss her and long to see her again, I know I can't. If I face her, I'll forget everything she did to me and forgive her, but I can't let that happen. Lying is where I draw the line.

The doorbell rings again. Twice this time. Stepping out of my bedroom, I trudge up to the front door. I take two deep breaths before swinging it open. But it's not Hazel who's standing on my porch.

"*Ah, ben tu es là!*" Matt says, brushing past me into the entryway. "What happened? You look terrible."

He's wearing his police uniform, which always makes him look older—and more mature—than he really is.

"What are you doing here?" I ask.

"Dude, your boss called because he thought you were dead or something. Apparently, you missed work these past couple of days."

A flush of adrenaline courses through me. "*Merde!* I completely lost track of time. Jean-Pierre is going to kill me." I meant to call in sick yesterday, but I must have forgotten.

"Yeah, he probably will," he says casually, sitting at the kitchen bar. "What happened? Wait. Have you been crying?"

I look away as I sink into the seat beside him. "No."

"Brother," Matt says, his voice now uncharacteristically soft. "Tell me what's wrong. It's not like you to miss work. What happened?"

I peer at him for a second, trying to gauge whether he's serious, but there's no mirth or malice in his eyes. "I broke up with Hazel."

"Oh, man. I'm sorry. What happened between you two?"

I swallow hard. "She lied to me. She pretended to be a historian, but she's actually a gastronomy critic for an American magazine." Saying the truth out loud twists the knife even further into my wounded ego.

His eyebrows shoot up. "And you broke up with her over that?"

I stare back at him, wrinkling my forehead. "Yes."

"Man," he says, shaking his head vehemently. "You're such a moron."

"Are you serious?" I fly from the kitchen stool and bang a fist on the bar. "She lied to me!"

"Chill, dude. She's a food critic, not an FBI agent who went undercover and seduced you to take down your family or something. And even *that* might be forgivable."

"Huh?" I blink back at him, confused. What on earth is he talking about?

"Well, that's what Agathe told me, at least. She reads too many novels if you ask me, but that's not the point. What I'm saying is, it's not that bad. I mean, honestly, she's pretty great. And yes, you dated, and she omitted the truth, but she probably couldn't tell you since you two met at the restaurant and she was there as a critic. I'm pretty sure those guys have a code or something."

I roll my eyes. "She doesn't work for the CIA, Matt."

"Still," he says with a shrug. "They probably don't want the chefs to know who they are, or it would blow the entire operation."

I shake my head at him, but he's got a point. "Still, after moving in with me, and after we started the whole dating thing, she could have said something. She had *plenty* of opportunities," I say, my throat going dry as images of those moments flash before my eyes again. "And by that time, she had already eaten at my place."

"Look, man," Matt says, placing a hand on my shoulder. "When you were together, I had never seen you so happy before. I didn't think you'd ever land a girlfriend again after the last disaster, and the fact that you brought her to Mom's birthday says a lot about how special she is. You should think twice about it."

My heart clenches at Matt's words. A few days ago, that was all true. Hazel did make me happy like no one else ever has. And she was special. Even in the beginning, it never really felt fake. I swallow the lump growing in my throat, looking away. "We weren't really dating then..." I mumble.

He frowns. "What?"

"We were faking it so Mom would get off my back about finding a girl." I breathe out a heavy sigh as I think back to that first night when I met Hazel. It feels like a lifetime ago, but really, it's only been two weeks. "Hazel was just a customer from the restaurant who needed a place to crash because the strike overcrowded the hotels. Mom was all over me about having Justine Gardinet come over for her birthday, and I panicked, saying I was seeing someone. Hazel agreed to come as a thank you."

Matt's jaw is practically on the floor. "Seriously?"

I arch an eyebrow. "Could I invent something so far-fetched?"

His frown deepens. "Maybe, if you were one of those authors my wife loves so much."

I raise an eyebrow.

"So, when did it start to become real?"

"For me, since the beginning. For her, I don't know if it ever was." The words might as well be sharpened knives because they're slicing my heart in two. "She said she wanted to be with me for real, and we talked about a future together. But I don't even think any of that was true."

"So, most of this thing was a lie?" Matt says, cocking his head. "Per your request."

Warmth rises to my cheeks. "Well, yes."

"*Aaaand* you're okay with that?" he asks with a pointed look.

I shake my head. "Look, I know where you're going with this, but it's not the same. What's gotten into you, playing the devil's advocate? What ever happened to brothers having each other's backs, huh?"

"Dude, that's exactly what I'm doing. My job, as your brother, is to make you see how much of a dumbass you are. And I think you're at a world-class level right now."

I throw him a death glare. "Shut up."

"Seriously, though. You sucked this girl into a fake dating relationship for Mom. You had her come to family functions when she doesn't even speak the language, help you out during the festival, and even kiss you. Basically, you made her fall in love with you one spoonful at a time. And *then,* when you learn a single lie she told you when you guys met, you throw it all away, even though you're clearly in love with her? Yup. World-class dumbassery, *mec.*"

"It's not some isolated little thing she lied about. It's her job. A huge part of who she is."

"Oh, because lying to Mom, to your entire family, is any smaller?"

I cross my arms over my chest. "It's not the same."

"Of course it is! You're just biased because you're hurt, and you always think nothing will go your way. You've got it in your brain that you're not ready to love again because of what Emeline did—which was extremely crappy, by the way. Yes, she took advantage of you and lied about it. That's a serious offense. What Hazel did? Not so much."

I stare down at the kitchen floor, concentrating on the heavy rise and fall of my breath. "It doesn't matter anyway. She's gone."

"Because you let her go."

I start pacing wildly. "She doesn't want to be here, Matt. Paris was a disappointment for her. She misses the Florida sun and her sister. She would have— "

"Ah, there it is," he cuts in, shaking his head. "You're just too scared to lose her, and you're afraid of getting hurt. That's why you rejected her first. Now we're getting somewhere."

"Oh, yeah, genius," I say with a fake smile. "Your interrogation techniques are through the roof."

I hate it when my brother is right. Especially when it concerns me. The fear of not being enough for Hazel is very real. What if we start building something, and she realizes it's not what she wants? That I'm not who she needs? What if she can't get over her hatred for the city?

I continue pacing, my mind working at double speed. This whole thing feels bigger than the fact that she concealed her job from me. How could it be, though? Lying is everything I hate, and I can't forgive that. Then again, one look at her, and I want to forgive her every misstep. Deep down, I know that she didn't have any ill intent, like Emeline did. I checked the website. My review is the last one she wrote, which means she didn't review the restaurants we visited together. And I'm certain she wrote it before she stayed with me, which is why I've been debating calling her. But does it really change anything? She did choose to stay with me afterwards, and she could have told me then. No, she *should* have told me, instead of lying to my face day after day. Not that she talked about her job much, but . . . My brain replays the moments when I spurred her to tell me about her work, and now I feel it, the awkwardness. How she changed the subject as quickly as possible and never brought it up herself. My heart tightens. I don't think she ever wanted to lie to me, and I know how it feels to get caught up in a lie, not knowing how to dig yourself out. To want a lie to become reality so badly it hurts.

I close my eyes, massaging my temples. These past couple of weeks have been a rollercoaster of emotions, but what if we could still have a happy ending? What if she loves me too? If she did, I would be a fool to let her go. To let *that* go, when I know what we had was special. In my heart, I know Hazel. And I know she just lied because she wanted this to be true just as much as I did. And who cares if she still hates Paris? I can live and cook anywhere in the world. As long as I'm with her, nothing else matters.

I don't even know why I didn't consider that possibility earlier. She doesn't have to stay. I can go.

"Dude, you're scaring me," Matt says, eying me warily.

"You're right," I finally say, swallowing. "I overreacted, and I have to talk to her. I need to get her back."

My heart leaps at the thought. I can almost see me there, sitting on her porch under the Floridian sun, kissing her and holding her tight.

"So, what are you going to do now? Hop on a plane to Florida? Do you need a police escort?"

I roll my eyes. Would showing up at her home really work? After how I treated her, it doesn't feel like enough. I was the one who jumped to conclusions. I didn't even give her the chance to explain, much less give her the benefit of the doubt.

"What if she's not interested?" I ask, my eyes downcast. The thought tightens its grip on my heart. Maybe it's too late. Wallowing for two days like an idiot, unable to see what was right in front of me, might have killed any chance of getting Hazel back. "I don't even know where she lives," I admit, sitting down on the couch, cradling my head in my hands. "And even if I do find her, she might not want anything to do with me."

"At least you'll know," Matt says, resting a hand on my shoulder. "It's better than spending your whole life wondering what could have been, right? As for the address, I'll see what I can find from the airport police. I can call in a favor."

"Really?" I ask, my pulse accelerating.

He smirks. "I should be able to sneak a glimpse at her contact address if I ask nicely."

I spring to my feet. "I guess I'm going to the airport."

He slaps my back. "I'd say good luck, but that would just jinx it so . . . *merde*. I'll work on that address and I'll text you."

With a smile so big it hurts, I grab my coat and run out of the house, my racing heartbeat matching my every step.

Chapter 26

Hazel

Once again, I'm waiting in line at the reservation desk, but I keep letting other people in front of me. I've been doing that for the last couple of days. I keep shuffling around the departure hall like a zombie, trying to decide between going back to Olivier to apologize and explain, or giving up and flying back home. Frankly, that's what I deserve. I lied to him. And given his history, I can't blame him for the way he reacted. I deserve the pain, the heartache. Yet I can't bring myself to make a decision. It's like my own brain is adding to the confusion, torturing me even more. And I know I've earned it.

I receive curious looks from the other travelers every time I step back in line, though now there's an additional hint of disgust. Granted, I haven't showered in two days, and I look like hell. The sink in the airport restrooms might actually be making me filthier every time I use it.

Frankly, besides the fact that I clearly enjoy torturing myself, I don't know why I'm still here. Waiting around won't change anything. It's not like Olivier is going to run into the terminal, all sweaty and searching for me because he loves me and doesn't want me to leave. I know I mentioned that my life was a romcom, but I've learned very well by now that I'm not the girl that gets the happy ending. Instead, I'm perpetually stuck at the beginning of the movie. And it's my own darn fault.

Yet somehow, I can't bring myself to walk up to that counter and schedule my flight home. Because the truth is, I don't want to go. Crazy, since I hated this city from day one. But things changed. Now, I want to stay. And I want Olivier.

No, I can't leave. Not until I've told him that I love him. What if those words could change his mind? Love is supposed to be one of the most powerful forces in the universe. If there was a rock-paper-scissors with love, I'm pretty sure love would trump everything else. Even lies. At least, that's what those cheesy romcoms try to teach us.

That's it. I've made up my mind. I'm going back. Whatever happens, I'm ending this story tonight—happy or not. If there's one thing this episode in life has taught me, it's that I have to be honest, with others and with myself, or I'll regret it for the rest of my life. So that's what I'll do. Even if it does twist the knife in my wounded heart.

I stumble over my suitcase as I try to back out of the line, apologizing to the three people who I've knocked aside in the process. Then, I speed-walk back to the metro station. I elbow my way across the platform, and when the train rolls up, I fight my way inside. Which is *not* an easy task when your suitcase is almost as big—and as heavy—as you. But there's no way I'm not catching this train. People curse in French at the rude American, but I couldn't care less.

I'm now scrambling like a maniac through the second station, where I'm going to catch the next line to Olivier's neighborhood. More French curses are spat at me as I run into people or hit them with my suitcase.

I'm wiping the sweat from my forehead when I collide with someone. But instead of a hard shock, the impact is soft and smells like cinnamon. And lemongrass.

My heart pounds harder as I raise my head, my eyes meeting Olivier's.

He opens his mouth at the same time as me. Then, he shakes his head, incredulous.

"What?"

"You?"

"What are you doing here?" we finally ask at the same time, and I bite my lip to contain my smile.

"I came back for you," I say, still catching my breath.

His lips tilt into a beaming smile, showcasing his delicious dimple. "Me too. I can't let you go, Hazel."

"I'm sorry I lied to you. I was there to critique your restaurant when we met, but I couldn't tell you. And then, you offered me a room, and it got complicated. But it's not who I am, and I'll never—"

He tucks a lock of sweaty hair behind my ear. "I know. I forgive you. And I overreacted. The whole thing brought up bad memories of my ex."

"You forgive me?" I breathe, my heart fluttering. "Are you sure?"

His eyes are brimming with sincerity. "Yes, I'm sure. You're nothing like her. I understand that. Please, Hazel, can I come with you?"

I do a double take. "What? To the US?"

He nods, cupping my face in his hands. "I can cook anywhere. As long as we're together, I'll be fine."

My heart explodes at his words. He's willing to leave his entire life behind—for me?

"But you love Paris," I say. "And your family is here."

He caresses my cheek softly. "All I need is you, Hazel. I don't want you to stay in a city you hate, just for my sake. And I wouldn't say no to some warm Floridian weather either," he adds with a chuckle.

That makes me smile. "But I don't hate Paris anymore. How could I when it's the place I found love?"

His features soften, and once again, I take in how beautiful this man is, even beneath the horrible fluorescent lights of the metro station. "You love me?"

I feel the blush heating up my cheeks. Maybe I should have held onto that or waited for him to say it first. But it's the truth, and I'm done lying to the man I love. "I do."

"I love you too," he breathes, sending my heart soaring on a bungee jump.

I tut. "*En français, s'il vous plait?*"

"*Je t'aime*, Hazel."

"Much better," I say, placing a hand on his chest. He covers it with his. "So, it looks like we're both in *loaf*, then?"

A smile is now slowly building on his face, but I don't give it time to reach his ears. Letting go of my suitcase, I throw my arms around his neck and kiss him. He lifts me up, and we kiss until we can't feel our lips anymore, our bodies seeming to melt into one person. One very happy person.

You know the scene at the end of a romcom, where the couple meets in the airport, and they finally make up and kiss?

Well, this isn't like that at all.

The corridor we're in smells like trash and urine, there's a gap-toothed homeless guy huddled on a blanket right next to us, and people keep bumping into us because we're in the middle of the way.

There is absolutely nothing romantic about this scene. But it doesn't matter.

Why would I need some fictional romance setting when I've got the real deal? In a way, this is even more perfect. I came to Paris with my head full of fantasies, but fantasies don't exist.

And let me tell you something. Reality is a whole lot better.

Epilogue

Olivier

"Are you nervous?" Hazel asks as we leave the metro. I want to say yes, but I know she's talking about the restaurant opening, and I'm not nervous about that.

"It's going to be great," she says, squeezing my hand.

"I know," I say with a smile, then bring her hand to my lips to plant a kiss on it. "We're ready."

I've got a fantastic sous chef, the place looks amazing, and the menu I've prepared for this week is inspiring. Needless to say, I'm pretty confident.

We arrive at our new restaurant that's nestled on a cute 6th arrondissement street. We named it Jeux de Mets which is a French pun. "Jeu de mot" means "pun" in French and "mets" means "dishes." Before entering, we stop in front of it to admire the navy-blue facade and the gorgeous flower arrangements, which are situated around the front door in standing and hanging planters. Hazel's doing, of course. She's played a huge role in the refurbishment of the space, but also in the creation of the menu. She even suggested we do a special event every week, and we've settled on four: *Escargot* day, *Grenouille* day, *Crêpe* day and even Kale day. But since it's the middle of October, tonight, we're showcasing the butternut gnocchi on the menu. The first dish we made together, and one of my new favorites.

We're doing a soft opening with only friends and family. Our first real service will be tomorrow. Even Ivy and her fiancé are coming. It'll be their first time in Paris, and I'm eager to finally meet them.

The dining room is not huge—sixty square meters—but it feels like home. The walls are painted in dark blue and beige, and the hardwood floors enhance the cozy at-home atmosphere we wanted to give this place. All around the room are speech bubbles with our favorite puns—in English and in French, since Hazel is getting so much better now. We even have a blackboard where people can add their own. Some of my personal favorites are "Robert *Brownie* Jr," "Not All Heros Wear *Crêpes*," and "*Cereal* Killer."

When I step into my brand-new kitchen, my heart swells with pride. Finally, after all this time, I'm doing this. My dad wasn't thrilled when I left the palace, and he hasn't been very supportive, but Mom said he's coming today. I hope I'll be able to change his mind.

"Your dad will love it," Hazel says, coming up behind me to give me a hug.

"Are you a mind reader?" I ask, turning to wrap her in my arms.

"Maybe."

"Well, I hope you're right."

"I am. You'll see," she says, nuzzling her head against my chest. "Let's start getting everything ready."

With a nod, I start pulling the supplies and ingredients out. We have to be particularly organized today, since it's only the two of us. But I'm relieved that we finally found a waiter and a dishwasher who will be joining us next week.

To make it easier on us, we're serving a tasting menu today. We start preparing everything for the full house we're expecting. I'm so in the zone, I nearly forget this is such a big day for me. Not because of the restaurant's opening, but because today could change everything for me. For us.

I steal a peek at Hazel, who's in charge of making the gnocchi. She's working with such diligence and care, a surge of pride overwhelms me. Sure, this is my restaurant, but she's the fuel behind it and the reason I'm confident it'll be a *franc* success.

Finally, we've prepared everything that could be made in advance, and we're ready for the big moment. The tables are set, and the stress is beginning to rise.

In a flash, we transform from a quiet restaurant with only the two of us to a full house bursting with smiling and encouraging faces. We're doing a stand-up *apéritif* before serving the food, and everyone is enjoying Luc's champagne.

"Brother," Matt says, stepping into the restaurant with Agathe and the girls not far behind. "This looks great." He slaps the back of my head and gives me a hug. He's already been here a couple of times, and even lent a hand, but he hasn't seen the finished product yet. No one has.

As we part, I'm smiling from ear to ear "*Merci*."

"*Où est Hazel*? And is there a rin—"

I quickly shush him, placing a hand over his mouth to stop him. Turning around, I realize with a wave of relief that Hazel is at the other end of the room, talking fast with her sister and her fiancé, Dan.

"Wait. Don't tell me you changed your mind?" Matt says, narrowing his eyes.

"Of course not. I just haven't done it yet."

"Hey," Agathe says, shuffling closer with the girls. I receive a new round of hugs, and she congratulates me before bombarding me with questions about the restaurant and what I have planned for today.

"Great turnout too," she says, looking around.

It is, and I'm grateful for everyone who came to support Hazel and me. Many of my chef friends are here, including Gabriel and Ludo. I also invited some of my staff from Cezanne, friends from school, cousins, uncles, and a few of my mom's friends. But my mom hasn't arrived yet.

I glance at the clock hanging on the wall. Twelve-forty. My mom is never late, especially not by forty minutes.

"They're coming," Agathe says, rubbing my back. "Your mom told me so again yesterday."

"I know," I mumble. I force a smile before turning around to talk with Ludo. I know she wouldn't miss this for the world. But I also know my father and the firm position he's held against me opening my own restaurant. I'm well aware how stubborn he can be. How stubborn they *both* are. And in my mind, I see them arguing over it. Her pushing for him to come and him refusing to. Then, a knot forms in my stomach. What if it's not that, but something that happened on their way over here?

I grab my phone from my pocket. But as I do, the bell on the front door jingles to indicate a new arrival. I glance over, and my heart leaps when I spot my parents on the threshold, my mom practically shoving my dad inside before closing the door behind her.

I make my way to the entrance, and Hazel is already in my mother's arms when I reach them.

"You came," I state, furrowing my eyebrows as I look at my dad. I still can't believe he's actually here.

He clears his throat, unzipping his coat. "Well, your mom made me come. And I wanted to see what you could do."

My eyebrows shoot up, and my heart rattles in my chest. "Really? I thought you disapproved."

"I do. But I have to try your food before I make a final judgment, don't I?" His voice is low and grumbled, but I hear every word loud and clear. How could I miss it? It's my dad's mantra. He's been teaching us to "try things before we hate them" our entire lives.

I nod, watching him as he strides into the dining room. He's immediately accosted by Ludo, and they start talking.

"He'll come around," Mom says, kissing me hello. "I'm proud of you, *mon fils*. And he'll be too."

Hazel laces her fingers with mine and gives me an encouraging look. "You'll make him proud."

I've never been so animated in the kitchen. Every crackle of food roasting in the pan, every warm aroma, every plate I garnish fuels me, and it's like there's a fire inside me I didn't know existed. A flame that's roaring with pleasure. Hazel is mostly serving today, and every time she comes back with words of praise, my heart booms in my chest, and pride overwhelms me.

"Everybody is loving it," she gushes, wrapping her arms around my waist. I turn around and pull her close, dropping a peck on her forehead, then her lips. She murmurs, "I told you we could never go wrong with crêpes for dessert."

"You were right. I *donut* know what I'd do without you," I say, holding her tighter.

A goofy smile lights up her beautiful lips, and I know her mind's already going a thousand miles an hour, trying to find a cute response.

But it'll have to wait. Because my dad is standing at the kitchen door, clearing his throat.

My pulse quickens, and Hazel must feel it, because she places her hand on my hammering chest for a second and gives me an encouraging look. Then, she smiles and leaves me alone with him.

My dad takes a few steps into the kitchen and looks around curiously. He opens his mouth, then closes it. I wonder if he's holding back on his criticisms or just doesn't know where to start. He ambles around the room, inspecting every inch of the kitchen, and my blood is now as cold as the ice cream I served with the crêpes.

Finally, I can't take it anymore. "What do—"

"You did good, Olivier," he says, his dark eyes now fixed on me. "You chose a good location, the kitchen is well-equipped, and the menu is well-thought out."

I pinch myself to make sure this is actually happening. "What about the food?" I ask, wringing my hands. "Did you like it?"

He pauses for a beat, and my stomach twists. I knew it was too good to be true. Then, he responds, "I did. The appetizer took me by surprise, I have to admit. It was a little bold to add the yuzu. It could have taken over."

"But it didn't," I venture, though it comes out like a question.

"No, it didn't," he says, his gaze piercing. "The gnocchi were made perfectly, and the sauce was smooth, provided in just the right amount. I also liked the play on the texture from the crushed nuts and the freshness that the parsley brought to the dish. Simple, but smart."

My eyes widen like two saucepans, and I keep pinching myself. I'm pretty sure it'll leave a nasty mark, but who cares? My dad liked my cuisine!

"I still think it's a waste not to have you working at a higher level," he grumbles, hands behind his back.

Here we go.

"And the crêpe soufflée technique could use some fine tuning, but there is potential, and I think you can be successful here. At least, that's what I hope for you."

I'm now holding onto the counter for support. "Really? I—thank you. I didn't think you'd like it, and you're right, there are a lot of things I could improve. Even the sauce. You said you liked it, but I think it's missing something. I just don't know what yet."

His mouth twists as he thinks it over. "Huh. Really? I thought it was perfect."

I press my lips together to hold back my smile, but it's too powerful and practically breaks my face in two.

My dad's face softens, and a ghost of a smile appears on his lips. "The crêpe soufflée technique, however . . ."

A chuckle bursts out of me. "Agreed."

"But it's nothing unfixable. Nine a.m. tomorrow. I'll help you."

"Yes, sir," I say with a nod, coming over to him with my hand outstretched. But to my utmost surprise, he pulls me into a hug.

Today was everything I ever hoped for. No, more. I never even dared to dream this big. But the pressure is still on, because the biggest moment is yet to come.

We're finishing cleaning up, and if Hazel is half as exhausted as I am, she doesn't show it. She's still beaming as she puts everything away with the same energy she had this morning.

I walk up to her, wrap my arms around her waist, and make her turn around to face me. She gasps in surprise.

"So, sous chef, did today live up to your expectations? What do you think of this new job?"

She giggles, her eyes sparkling. "It was amazing. I always knew I wanted to work with food, but I didn't know I could actually be good at it. And I was, right?"

I chuckle, drawing her even closer. "Of course you were. The best sous chef I've ever had. You're very talented. You belong in the kitchen. With me."

She kisses me softly on the lips. "That's never been clearer than today. It didn't even seem like work."

I know the feeling. It never feels like work for me either. Not when I'm cooking my own cuisine. Cooking is a passion, and working from your passion is pretty much an endless vacation. "I need to ask you something," I say, swallowing hard as I fidget with the corner of my pocket. "It can't wait."

A frown clouds her perfect features. "Okay."

"Hazel," I say, dropping to one knee. Her eyes widen, and her mouth parts slightly. Well, at least she's not running away. So far, so good. "I've never been happier than since the moment you chased me down that street in your stilettos." Smiling, I pause to remember that night. Because that's when everything changed.

She chuckles, shaking her head lightly. I continue, "You've helped me fall back in love with cooking, and you captured my heart along the way. I could never imagine a life without you. I'm *nuts* about you, and I love you *s'more* and *s'more* every day," I add, fighting a face-splitting grin. I'm relieved when I see that her expression matches mine. I pull the small box from my pocket and open it in front of me. "Will you please marry me?"

Wetting her lips, she leans down and says, *"Oui.* My heart *beets* for you, Olivier. *Lime* all yours."

Darn. I love this girl so much.

Laughing, I lift her up into my arms and kiss her with everything in my soul. Looks like fall is our season of love after all.

Not ready to say goodbye to Olivier and Hazel yet? Get a glimpse of their *apple*-y ever after in the extended epilogue!

And if you want to fall for more delicious romcoms, keep reading to fill your TBR with more swoony stories from the Cinnamon Rolls & Pumpkin Spice series!

Already looking forward to winter?

Me too! Ski, Sparks, & Serendipity is a grumpy sunshine small town romcom with winter vibes, ski lessons and lots of adorable huskies.

Releases December 6th. Preorder Now!

Read the rest of the Cinnamon Rolls and Pumpkin Spice Series!

Each book is a standalone, full-length, closed-door romance that can be read in any order.
Hating the Cinnamon Roll CEO by Camilla Evergreen
Falling for Autumn (Again) by Jen Atkinson
Paris, Pumpkins & Puns by Marion De Ré
Fall With Me by Amanda P. Jones
Cinnamon & Spice Conundrum by Leah Busboom
Cinnamon Roll Set Up by Genny Carrick

PARIS, PUMPKINS & PUNS

Coffee Break with the Billionaire by Holly Kerr
The Friendly Fall by Kristine W. Joy

A NOTE FROM MARION

Ah! This book. This one is special. It came to me as my good friend Camilla and I were talking about doing a multi-author series last summer and I immediately fell in love with the story. As the only French writer in the group, I felt it was my duty to write a story in France. Haha.

Well, it won't be my last.

I had so much fun with this one: the clichés, the puns, the mix of French and English and the gastronomy aspects. As a foodie, it was the perfect story for me to write.

I hope you had a *pun*-tastic time reading this one! And if you're not ready to say goodbye to these characters, good news! Ivy is getting her own story, and her own season: winter!

Au revoir et à bientôt!

Acknowledgements

This book was so much fun to write and I want to give a special thanks to all the people who allow me to make my dream come true every day: writing stories and sharing them with all of you! Ten books!

First, I *wonton* thank my friend **Camilla Evergreen** for doing this with me. You did a fantastic job running this multi-author series and the *raisin* it's been such a wonderful adventure. Thank you so *mochi* for being a great friend!

Thank you to the ladies of the Cinnamon Rolls & Pumpkin Spices series, **Jen**, **Amanda**, **Leah**, **Genny**, **Holly** and **Kristine**. I *loafed* doing this with you and I'm so *egg*-cited to count you as my friends.

I'd like to thank **Brooke**, the *grate*-st editor of all *thyme*! Thank you for sticking by me and helping me grow as a writer with every single book!

A big fat thank you to **Allie**, my a-*maize*-ing beta reader. Thank you for loving Olivier so much and for making me a *butter* storyteller. I'm so *grape*-ful for you.

Meghan, thanks a *melon* for polishing my manuscript and for your everlasting support. *Lime* so happy to have you in my corner.

Thank you to **Noria** at House of Orian for this brew-ti-ful cover.

Yvette, Elizabeth, Melissa, Patty, Katie, Amanda, Devika, Brittany, Evy, Susan, and **Tammy**, thank you for being part of my **Sparkling Street Team**, and for being my number one fans and cheerleaders. I'm *soy* thankful for each and every single one of you and words cannot express *hummus* I love you!

My awesome **Advanced Readers**, thanks a *brunch* for helping me spread the word about my books, and catching the last typos! You're *shrimply* the best!

Cathy, a huge thank you for helping me with the admin stuff, allowing me to spend more time on my writing. I *donut* know what I'd do without you.

A massive thank you to the **Bookstagram** community. You guys must know by now how much I *clove* you by now. But I'll say it again, just in *queso* someone missed the memo! Thanks for *bacon* such pretty posts about my books and supporting indie authors.

To my husband, **Etienne**. Thanks for *pudding* up with me. Being married to a writer isn't always easy. I'm *nuts* about you and I love you *s'more and s'more* every day.

A mes **parents**, un grand merci pour votre soutien! Malheureusement, je n'ai pas trouvé de jeu de mots en français! Pathétique, non?

And to my **readers**, thank you for your messages, social media posts and review. I appreciate you *berry* much and I *yam* so thankful for you. I still can't *brie*-live this is my job sometimes. Thank you for allowing me to do *eat*.

ALSO BY MARION DE RÉ

All the books in the Season of Love series:

Paris, Pumpkins & Puns

Ski, Sparks & Serendipity

To find the complete list of books by Marion De Ré:

If you want help finding your next favorite books, try the TBR Generator!

ABOUT THE AUTHOR

Marion De Ré is a French national with an American heart. She lives in the French countryside with her husband, Etienne, and her cat, Caline. Growing up with books and being passionate about the English language, she naturally started to write stories in English. You can expect all your beloved tropes in her writing as well as a good dose of humor, and all the feels. When she's not reading or writing, you can find her on a plane to a far-away destination or in a Champagne cellar, indulging in a tasting of her favorite drink.

Marion loves hearing from her readers. Visit her website www.marionderewrites.fr and sign up for her newsletter to be the first to know about her upcoming books and for exclusive content.

You can also find her on social media:

Facebook and Instagram: @marionderewrites

Hang out with Marion in her exclusive book club! Find all the links here:

Connect with Marion

Printed in Great Britain
by Amazon